The
Wilder
Doctrine

SM Dougan

http://smdougan.com

The Wilder Doctrine is a work of fiction. The incidents, names, places and characters are the product of the author's imagination and any resemblance to actual persons, living or dead, businesses, locations or events are completely coincidental.

This book is dedicated to my family, and friends who's personalities and conversations have given my imagination fuel to create.

My deepest thanks to you all.

Chapter 1

A sharp spike of pain ripped from the bottom of the young man's foot through his body and jolted him awake. Searching for the source of the pain, he saw the shadowy figure of an old man with a cane turning to walk away. The young man knew immediately that it was that cane that had struck him awake.

Before the young man could utter a word, the old man's voice boomed, "Get out of bed, boy! You are wasting this day! Your breakfast is getting cold!" With that the old man exited the bedroom.

The young man shook his head as he surveyed the room. It was old and run down with well seasoned and oddly cut planks cladding the walls and floor. It was clean though, and didn't have the musty smell of old buildings. Still, he was sure this place had been standing for a very long time.

As he swung his feet to the ground he saw he was naked. He spotted a pile of clothes neatly folded on a nearby chair. He reached for them and as he did so he realized for the first time since waking that nothing in this room, nor the old man who had so rudely awakened him, was familiar to him.

The visions that he had so deeply enjoyed only moments ago swept over him again. He realized sadly, they were only a dream. They had been a place of warmth and light; a place his mind had created solely for him and not at all like this place.

The peace and comfort he had felt in his slumber was not something he could imagine feeling in the reality of here. The visions had seemed so real. Even now, fully awake, he believed it to be a place he had been, although he knew that wasn't possible.

As he dressed in the white tunic and thick belt, his eyes continually scanned all that surrounded him. The light of morning pierced the film of dirt on the window and created a pleasant glow in the room. The room itself contained very little. The pieces of furniture that did exist, although old and handmade, were sturdy, simple and functional.

Having finished dressing, the young man pulled his long hair into a ponytail, stretched his arms over his head, and slowly walked into the main area of the building. It, too, was sparse in its appointments.

A large stone fireplace took up most of the wall across from the young man's room. Between his door and the fireplace was a table built of hand hewn timbers. The remainder of the space was decorated with a few chairs and some shelving stocked with only the most basic of necessities. The whole building couldn't be described as any more than a cabin.

The young man continued towards the table and the single plate of food that rested on it. Just passed the table was the old man crouched low, stocking the fire. The blackened iron caldron was swung clear, waiting for the next meal it would house. As the young man sat, he continued to examine the space. Everything he saw appeared familiar at a very impersonal level. It was a familiarity in identification but he knew this place was not his home. He wasn't sure where he was, but he knew it wasn't home. He searched his memory again and again, but all that came was the light and warmth of his dream. He shook off the empty feeling that fell over him as quickly as he could.

Before he began to eat, the young man looked to the old man, "Are you not eating?"

The old man stood slowly with a light grunt and as he turned towards the young man, he barked unpleasantly, "No!", and he strolled slowly to the table. His voice sounded old indeed and the ice blue of his eyes pierced past his dark, heavily wrinkled skin. His face was framed by long grey hair and beard and he wore a tattered, old deep brown robe. As the old man came close, the young man spoke again. His voice, cautious and unsure, "I'm afraid I don't recall your name? Or what this place is. Or even what my own name is."

The old man's laugh was deep and the young man felt it within his own belly. When the laughter ceased, the old man looked deep into the young man's blue eyes with an intensity that threatened to turn the warmth of the young man's eyes as icy as his own. His facial expression turned so deep that it didn't look real.

When he finally spoke, his voice boomed, "You are nothing! You are no one! You, young lad, are whatever I say you are!"

An evil grin spread across the old man's face, "I am someone that you will get to know very well soon enough. You will learn to trust me and you will learn to hate me. Call me, Dominus."

Dominus slammed his cane down hard on the table in front of the young man. The sound of it made the young man jump noticeably. The old man spoke again with the same loud and cavernous voice as he slapped the young man across the side of the head, "Eat!"

Dominus smiled deliberately and unpleasantly for a moment before he rose from the table and walked out of the small cabin.

The young man felt the blood leave his face and fear engulf the pit of his stomach. He quickly shook his head to regain focus, and then chuckled nervously under his breath as he rubbed his hand over the light whiskers that protruded from his cheeks, chin and neck, "Crazy old man."

He brushed his long brown hair back in a bunch and tied it with a small piece of twine before he began to eat.

When he finished the meal, he left the table and stared at the empty plate for a moment. He knew how much food had been on the plate and he knew how full he felt. He was certain he had eaten far more than the plate had contained. He shrugged it off and walked out the open door of the cabin and into the daylight.

The warmth of the sun felt fabulous as it sat just over the treetops. Surveying his surroundings, the young man determined the cabin itself was situated in the middle of a clearing of several acres. The ground housed thin grasses less than a foot tall. All of this was surrounded by a very dense, dark forest.

The young man could hear the sound of wood being chopped close by. He stretched his arms high above his head again before starting towards the source of the sound. He also heard the faint sound of a small stream flowing nearby, and birds and other sounds of nature all pleasantly wrapped together to create a comfortably pleasant ambiance of peace.

As he reached the back of the cabin, he saw a small paddock that contained a cow and a couple pigs. A small barn stood just beyond that. A dozen chickens wandered around and an exceptionally large black cat sat on a post supervising everything.

Next to the pen was a small, well established vegetable garden which appeared to be half way through its growing season.

Just past that, he could see Dominus splitting firewood. The pile waiting to be split wasn't more than a dozen pieces or so. Without turning or stopping, Dominus spoke without emotion, "Was the meal satisfactory, boy?"

The young man nodded to the back of Dominus' head, "Yes. Thank you. It was surprisingly tasty."

The young man hesitated for a moment before speaking again, "I don't like being called *boy*. What is my real name?"

The axe in Dominus' hand came down hard splitting the piece of wood sitting on the chopping block. As the axe head buried itself in the block, Dominus turned to face the young man. His face didn't appear angry and sweat trickled like rivulets through the crevices that lined his face, "As I have already told you, you are no one. You are nothing. You will listen to every word I say and you will do whatever I say without hesitation or question. That is all you need to know for the time being. Is that understood?"

The young man took immediate offence and spoke loudly, "Listen, old man. I know I am not some small child. I am a man. I don't know for sure, but I would guess in my early twenties. What are you, like a hundred or something? I have no idea who you are or where I am, but I'll be damned if I am going to let some shriveled up old man tell me what to do!"

Dominus smiled and grunted unpleasantly, "You, young lad, have no idea how wrong you are, and damned is what you may well be."

Dominus hesitated a moment before continuing, "I have seen many boys like you come and go. I was a wise guy, too, when I was a lad. I was taught well by another *old man*. I learned a great many things from him during the years of his life. When he moved on, I took over for him.

"For now you will live and you will learn a great many things from me. You will do as I say, period. This is not open for discussion." Dominus chuckled, "And you will thank me for it, and for the protection I provide."

The young man laughed out loud, "That's your story?" He chuckled again.

Dominus wasn't amused, "It won't be long before you fully understand my meanings, and trust me, you will understand."

He hesitated for a moment before continuing, "So tell me, boy, what was the last thing you did before going to bed last night, or tell me anything you did yesterday? Do you recall anything at all?"

The young man started to speak, but stopped. He was silent as he searched his vacant memory.

Dominus nodded knowingly, "I didn't think so. You will have a name in due course and I will be the one to give it to you, and I won't care if you happen to like it or not. Until then, you will only be known as *boy*, and you will answer to that immediately."

With an evil smile, Dominus handed the young man the axe, "Finish this up. I need to walk. I have talked to you as much as I care to, for now."

The young man looked at the out-stretched axe in Dominus' hand for a few brief moments before he took it. He held it in his own hands for a few seconds before tossing it aside. His stare never left the old man's eyes.

Dominus smiled, his gaze also fixed on the young man. He reached his hand out and instantly the axe reappeared within his grasp. He spoke with distinct sarcasm, "I believe you dropped this, *boy*."

The shock on the young man's face was clear as his defiant stare left Dominus' eyes in favor of the axe in Dominus' hand. Just as quickly he looked to the ground where he had tossed the axe. There was nothing there but ground.

The young man returned his attention to Dominus, "How did you do that?"

Dominus turned buried the axe in the top of the splitting block. Then he chuckled lightly and headed off towards the forest. The young man watched him until he was well out of sight before he turned to the pile of wood.

He gasped out loud. He was certain there had only been a dozen or so pieces of wood waiting to be split, but now the pile was easily six or seven times that size. His head snapped back in the direction Dominus had gone and stared into the darkness of the forest for a few moments. Then he returned his focus to the woodpile. He sighed again as he removed the axe from the block and began splitting.

Many hours passed. The light of day slowly gave way to the spectacular colors of dusk. The young man had finally finished splitting and neatly stacking the last of the wood. It had seemed the more he split, the more wood there was. It was as if the pile grew as needed to keep him busy all day. He shook his head, not wanting to accept that notion, and yet he couldn't deny what he had seen.

He believed a great many other facts coming his way would be equally hard to accept. He buried the head of the axe in the chopping block before gathering an armful of wood to take inside.

As he started walking past the garden and around the cabin to the door, he looked towards the woods where Dominus had gone hours ago. There was still no sign of him. The young man was surprised that he was actually starting to worry about the old man.

As he crossed the threshold of the cabin, the pungent stench of heavy beer filled his nostrils. Dominus was seated at the long table eating a plate of food. The breakfast plate the young man had left on the table in the morning was nowhere to be seen.

The young man walked passed Dominus and dumped the wood unceremoniously beside the fireplace. Then he sat at the table across from Dominus. Dominus didn't look up from his meal and neither man said a word for several minutes. Dominus ate quietly and the young man stared at him.

Finally the young man broke the silence, "When did you get back? I didn't see you come in. I thought you would have at least told me you were back."

Dominus' head was cast downwards as he ate, but he raised his eyes enough to look into the young man's face, "I am not accountable to you, boy. You are accountable to me. That is the way it is."

Dominus returned his attention to his food and the young man continued staring at him. Dominus finished his meal and as he dropped his fork on the plate, he looked up at the young man, "I went for a few pints. I have been back for about an hour. I ate my meal, period, end of story. I see you finished splitting the wood. Good."

The young man was annoyed, "Yes. Your precious wood is split. You are welcome."

Dominus laughed as he made a fist in front of the young man's face. He held it there for a few seconds for effect before he swung his arm towards the fireplace. A ball of bright orange and yellow left the end of his arm and burst into a pleasant fire in the fireplace, "The firewood isn't for me. I have no need of such things."

The shock on the young man's face was clear. Dominus belly laughed. Then Dominus pointed a finger at each candle and lantern in the room, and each lit in succession as easily as the fire.

The young man's immediate shock passed quickly and he looked at Dominus with a sneer. With distinct sarcasm, the young man spoke, "I'm impressed old man. Nice parlor trick. What do you do for an encore?"

Dominus, with a knowing smile, pointed at the table in front of him. Just as instantly as the various flames lit, a plate of food appeared in front of the young man. The young man sat back with a start and Dominus chuckled, "Eat boy, we will talk later."

The young man stared at the old man. He wanted to say something but didn't know where to start. Dominus reached across the table and smacked him on the side of his head, "Eat!"

The young man shook his head, "I don't know what is going on here. I don't know who you are, but I have no intention of just sitting here and putting up with this."

With that the young man rose swiftly from his chair.

Dominus was stoic, "Really? You have had enough have you? So be it. There is the door. There is nothing keeping you here. My life will continue the same whether you are here or not. I truly couldn't care less. There are others that will waste far less of my time."

The young man stared at Dominus for a moment with anger etched in his face. He wanted to say something, anything, but his anger prevented any words. He turned abruptly and headed for the door.

Dominus spoke immediately, "You should at least eat something before you go. You have no idea how long it will be before your next meal."

The young man ignored him and continued through the door and into the dusk. He maintained a steady pace as he walked his course towards the woods in the distance. The path Dominus had taken earlier was still clearly visible.

Dominus said he had gone for a couple pints so there must be a village or something down that path. With every step he took, the young man could hear Dominus laughing behind him.

Thankfully the sound of it diminished the further away from the cabin he got.

The young man hesitated momentarily as he reached the edge of the forest and looked back towards the cabin. He shook his head angrily before he continued into the forest. He didn't make it more than thirty feet before he walked into something hard. He was stopped abruptly and looked hard into the forest directly in front of him. The way was clear. There was nothing visible in front of him. He shook his head lightly then reached out his hand. It didn't travel far before it slowly began to vanish from sight.

He pulled it back quickly and inspected it. Satisfied it was still indeed attached, he tried again. Again, as it reached the same distance in front of him, his hand and arm disappeared. Again he retrieved it quickly and inspected it. Satisfied all was well, and knowing there was no pain he approached the same spot again, this time, head first.

As his head went through the unseen barrier, his eyes closed and after a quick second he opened them again. Before him the forest he had seen was gone. Instead, he now faced absolute blackness. He reached his hand in and put it in front of his face, but he couldn't see it. He drew it closer and closer until it touched his nose. It was a blackness of such depth that he knew it was not somewhere he wanted to venture. He quickly retreated and the forest reappeared in front of him.

The young man looked back towards the cabin. He growled angrily to himself before returning his attention to the forest in front of him. A moment passed before he left the path and began walking into the forest to his left. He headed into the more densely vegetated part of the forest. A few yards from the path, he once again tried walking forward with his hand stretched out in front of him. Again, at about the same distance, his hand vanished from sight. He retracted it again quickly.

He looked towards the cabin again before walking another forty feet further away from the path. The sky and the forest continued to grow darker around him. The dim light of the cabin was still visible in the distance. As dim as it was, the cabin light was sufficient for him to maintain his bearings.

Now much further from the path, he once again moved forward with his arm stretched out. And again, it vanished. He retrieved it more slowly this time and stared into the darkness in disgust. He realized that as much as he didn't want to go back, there was nowhere else for him to go.

That thought disturbed him even more. He couldn't imagine a place where such life could exist and yet be surrounded by absolute nothingness. This forest, the clearing and the cabin all were as real as he was. He knew that much without question. At the same time, he couldn't help but wonder how was it possible to be here and yet be completely surrounded by nothing. He searched his memory and could not recall any place other than this, but even still, this existence made no sense to him.

The young man then remembered what Dominus had said earlier, *'For now you will live and you will learn a great many things from me. You will thank me for it, and for the protection I provide.'* With a defeated sigh, the young man turned and walked slowly out of the forest towards the light of the cabin.

Thirty feet from the cabin, the small barn caught his attention. He stopped and looked at it for a moment, then back towards the cabin. He smiled to himself, "Fine. I think it is time for *you* to worry about *me*, old man."

The young man altered his course and headed towards the small barn instead. He was certain he could find some hay or something to make into a bed. There is a pig so there is a good chance there is still some food in the trough for him to eat. He knew whatever food there was, wouldn't be pleasant, but it would do.

Passing through the paddock, he stopped at the trough and grabbed a handful of mush. He pulled it towards his face. The smell was disgusting and he looked at it doubtfully. He recognized much of the individual foods in it, so he took a deep breath, pushed the handful passed his lips and swallowed as hard and as fast as he could. The flavor wasn't pleasant, but it wasn't as bad as he had expected. He managed to get it down and to keep it down.

Near the trough was some water and he dropped to his knees and quickly drank as many handfuls as possible to clear his mouth. Returning to his feet, he shook his head and turned towards the barn.

Walking in, he could see that there was not much to it. There was, however, a loft and it looked as though there was hay piled up there. Climbing up the makeshift ladder, and making his way to the pile of hay, he fashioned himself an area he would call a bed. Satisfied with his creation, he lay down and quickly fell asleep.

Chapter 2

A loud, deep thud woke the young man with a start. Quickly realizing where he was and the direction the sound came from, he looked over the edge of the loft. Below him Dominus was laughing and forcibly jamming a pitchfork into the boards of the loft. Dominus' voice was sarcastic, "Good. You're awake."

Dominus chuckled again and placed the pitchfork deliberately against a post before returning his attention to the young man, "You sure showed me didn't you? I hope your sleep in the hay was pleasant and your feast of pig slop was delectable."

He continued to chuckle, "Me, I sat in my chair in front of the fire enjoying the quiet. I savored a nice, sweet pipe and a few pints of ale before going to my nice, comfortable bed for a good night's sleep. I slept like a log."

Dominus laughed again, "Get up, boy! Feed the animals and clean the stalls. When you are finished, clean up and go inside. Your dinner from last night is still on the table. We don't waste food here. I expect it to be eaten."

Dominus turned to leave, but stopped and looked back up at the young man, "Oh, next time you decide you want to punish someone, pick something that will cause them more displeasure than it causes you."

Dominus laughed heartily but his voice quickly turned serious, "Now, get up and get on with it. You have a lot to do today. Lazing around in bed isn't allowed here either."

He turned away from the young man and left the barn.

The anger on the young man's face was clear and he wanted to scream. He knew it was pointless. No one other than himself, Dominus and these animals would hear it and of them all, he was the only one that would care. He sighed instead and climbed down from the loft.

On the ground, he reached for the pitchfork Dominus had held only moments ago. He smiled when he picked it up and looked out the barn doors. As he held the pitchfork firmly in both hands, he thrust it three times towards the door opening. He heard a deep laugh from Dominus in the distance.

The sound of his laughter infuriated the young man even more. He tossed the pitchfork aside and stomped out of the barn, heading for the door of the cabin. The door was open to the morning's fresh air and he walked straight through. Dominus was sitting at the long table eating.

The young man walked up to the table and stared across at Dominus.

Dominus casually lifted his head to make eye contact. His expression was empty, "Is there something you wish to say to me, boy?"

The young man took a deep breath, "I am not your slave, old man. I will not do your work for you. I want answers. I want them now. I want to know what this place is and how I can get out of here."

Dominus smiled as he casually pushed his plate of food aside. He thought for a moment before he spoke. When he did his voice was without emotion. He simply talked as if stating obvious facts, "This place is either your beginning or your end. That is a decision only you can make. You want answers, do you? For every answer there are only more questions. It will not matter what answers I give you, they would only lead to more questions. You are the only one that can answer your questions. All I can do is show you the way and you have to decide from there; all of reality boils down to *Yes* and *No*.

"That is all there is. For each question there is a result. That result is your result, no one else's.

Your fate, your destiny, your very existence boils down to you and *Yes* or *No*. So, what is this place? It is the same as every other place, a place of questions. What happens next is the result of your answers. So, you can believe what I have told you and do what I say, or you don't." Dominus paused for a moment before continuing, "You are what you do. So what will it be, boy, here with me, or out past the forest?"

Dominus stared into the young man's eyes. The young man returned the stare and could see that there was no emotion on Dominus' face and his eyes looked very deep and empty.

Finally the young man looked down at the table at the plate of food sitting there. He looked up at Dominus again and then snorted angrily, but turned and left the cabin.

Entering the barn, he shook his head and picked up the pitchfork. With a sigh he turned toward the first stall. This was the first time since waking that he realized how stiff and sore he was. Apparently the sleep in the loft was not as comfortable as he had imagined it would be. Nonetheless, he would be very sure not to let Dominus know how hurt he was.

After a few hours he completed his chores and washed up near the water pump before going into the cabin. Dominus was nowhere to be seen.

As promised, however, the meal that had appeared the night before remained in the same spot on the table.

It didn't look as appetizing this morning as it had last night. Hunger however won over and he began to eat. The slop last night served its purpose, but was hardly a meal, and the efforts of the morning combined to create a significant will to eat.

He ate quickly, but unlike the meal yesterday morning, this one didn't appear to grow as he ate. All that appeared to be on the plate when he sat was all the food the plate contained. He thought that perhaps what he had experienced yesterday was indeed just his imagination. But today he wished it would replenish as yesterday's had.

With the food finished, he left the table and took his plate to the caldron for a refill. He stared into it with disbelief. It was empty. He had been certain there would be more food, but there was none, and he wanted more.

He scanned the cabin for Dominus, but he was still nowhere in sight. He grunted in disgust and sharply placed the plate back on the table as he walked to the door. He was startled by the form of Dominus standing there.

Dominus didn't hesitate, "Are you looking for me, boy? Did you want more food? Pity."

With that Dominus pushed past the young man and into the cabin. He walked over to his chair beside the fireplace and sat down. He casually picked up his pipe, stuffed and lit it. The whole time the young man stood motionless, looking at him.

Dominus took a few draws from his pipe before he looked up towards the young man, "You still there? What is it? Do you wish to kill me, boy?" Dominus laughed, "Do you think you are the first one to want to do that? What will you do if you are successful?"

Dominus took a draw from him pipe before continuing, "Trust me, you will get your chance just the same. In fact I should expect that you will get several chances."

A silence lasted several moments. Then Dominus spoke again, "No, eh? Not yet at least. Fair enough. Fetch some water. We will need enough to fill half this caldron. We will need some firewood, too. Get enough wood for now and some for later. I expect it will be chilly tonight."

The young man didn't move and his expression remained unchanged.

Dominus stared at him for a few moments

before shrugging. He turned away from the young man and sank comfortably deeper in his chair.

A few more minutes passed before the young man turned away from Dominus and walked out the door. His mind raced with images of anger and vengeance. He could feel hate growing stronger within him. He didn't like how it felt in general, but at the same time he embraced it.

Instead of going to the pump, he walked over to a circle of handmade chairs twenty yards from the front door of the cabin. He chose one of the chairs that faced away from the cabin and he sat.

In front of him was the forest. It looked very dark. Somehow it looked even darker than it had yesterday. He shook that thought off and accepted that it was probably just a case of his own anger clouding his vision.

Time passed slowly as he sat motionless in the chair and stared into the forest. He felt the sun passing over head and eventually settling towards the east. That thought startled him. He looked skyward. Everything he felt and saw around him suggested the cardinal points, but all those assumptions must be wrong. There is no way they could be right, the sun sets in the west, not the east. Yet as he looked around, it was clear that it was indeed towards the east that the sun headed.

He shook his head again as he looked over his shoulder at the cabin, "I guess that is just one more reality that doesn't make sense here, eh, old man?"

His question had been muttered under his breath, but Dominus responded through the closed door of the cabin, "Yes, boy. A great many things appear to be what they are not. Everything you know as fact is as wrong as it can be. You will learn. I will teach you.

"The hate you are feeling now will also prove to be false, in spite of what you might think. The reality is that it is not me you actually hate, but yourself. This you will understand eventually too."

With that, the sky suddenly blackened. There was no pleasant transition from daylight through dusk and into night as one would expect. It was simply a stark and drastic change from light to night.

The sudden transformation startled him, but not as deeply this time. He was slowly accepting the unexplainable. He felt he was learning. Surprise can only happen when things happen that one is not expecting. Reality can take many different forms and is rarely exactly as one expects. Eliminate assumptions and surprises end.

The thought had no sooner cleared his mind when he heard Dominus' laughter from the cabin again. He shook his head in anger but still he didn't move; didn't comment; didn't respond in any way. He was determined to simply enjoy the pleasantness of the evening.

Time passed and as it did the temperature began to drop. The young man began to consider moving inside. Snow started falling. The sight of the snow surprised him, but only for a moment as he understood why. He realized that he would need to take in some wood to build a fire. He was angry again. Then he thought about the water, and his anger built.

The last thing he wanted was to appear as if he was yielding to Dominus' wishes. At the same time he knew these things were logical and he could do them if he could convince himself that he was doing it as a decision he made, opposed to the wishes of Dominus.

He stewed quietly for a few more moments before the silence of the night was broken by the screech of some great beast. Given the pitch and volume of the sound it could only have come from a large creature. The sound of it was like nothing he could recall ever hearing before.

The sound startled him and fear immediately gripped him. His head spun in the direction the sound seemed to be coming from. He strained his ears and eyes in an attempt to identify the source. Then the screech came again but from a completely different direction and he spun in the chair to look in that direction. Quickly another screech came from an entirely different direction, and then all became quiet again.

The young man looked all around and could not see anything that wasn't there before. After a few minutes other sounds began to emanate from the forest. He was certain the screeches had come from the sky, but now these sounds were clearly at ground level.

He stared hard into the forest, trying to catch a glimpse of anything that may be the source of the sounds. As hard as he tried, his eyes could not capture an image of anything through the darkness. As time passed the volume and number of sounds continued to grow. Initially the sounds had just been in front of him, now they seemed to be in all the woods that surrounded the cabin. Finally the noises became too loud for him to remain calm. He stood up and headed through the door of the cabin.

Dominus looked up casually from his chair, "Where's the water and firewood?"

The young man pointed outside and was about to speak, but stopped. He knew any comments he made would be pointless. He sighed and walked back out the door to the wood pile, the whole while scanning the forest line as the sounds continued unabated.

Gathering a large armful of firewood, he returned inside. He dropped the wood beside the fireplace and immediately went back outside with the water pail. He returned quickly with the water. He closed and locked the cabin door, hoping that would be sufficient to keep whatever was out there from coming in. Dominus simply nodded his thanks.

Satisfied the door was secure the young man proceeded to start a fire in the fireplace. Neither he nor Dominus said a word. He knew Dominus was capable to starting the fire with a flick of his wrist, but that was assistance the young didn't want.

The fire grew quite pleasantly and warmth quickly radiated throughout the small room. The young man smiled lightly as he took a chair beside the fire.

It was several minutes before Dominus broke the silence, "A tad noisy out there tonight was it?" Then he chuckled lightly.

The young man nodded, but didn't offer any words. Dominus returned the nod without saying anything further.

Satisfied the fire was burning well, the young man added a few more logs to ensure it would burn long into the night, then started towards his bedroom.

Dominus allowed him to walk up to the bedroom door before he spoke, "Where do you think you are going, boy?"

The young man looked back towards Dominus and pointed to the bedroom door, "I'm turning in. I'm tired."

Dominus spoke sharply, "The barn was good enough for you last night, I'm sure it will be fine for you again tonight."

The young man protested, "Alright. I'm sorry. I had a tantrum. I learned my lesson, okay. I'm turning in now."

Dominus spoke sharply again, "It is fine that you are apologizing, but you shouldn't have done anything that would give reason for an apology.

"You wish to turn in, that is fine, but this is my home and you are not welcome to sleep under my roof tonight. The barn will serve you again."

The young man was annoyed, "Oh come on. I said I was sorry. How long are you going to punish me?"

"I am not punishing you, boy. This is simply the way it is. Sleep in the barn. Tomorrow I may be more generous, but tonight you sleep in the barn."

The young man looked away from Dominus and started towards the cabin door. The sounds in the forest seemed to have increased in intensity and volume. Slowly he returned his gaze to Dominus and spoke softly, "I said I was sorry and I meant it. I will be more respectful. I just need some sleep."

Dominus laughed, "I see. Last night was quiet and safe. You hated me and sought revenge, so it was fine to sleep in the barn and eat pig slop.

"Tonight there are noises and sounds from beings you can't see or identify. Now you are afraid of what may happen to you out there. So now I am forgiven and you wish to share the protection I provide."

Dominus paused for a moment before continuing, "You are afraid because you do not know what is out there. You do not know what might happen. Your fear is based entirely on your imagination with no basis in reality. You may be safe in the barn, you may not. The only certainty at this point is you are not welcome to share my home. The rest is yet to be determined."

The young man snorted and turned towards the bedroom door. Dominus vanished from his chair and reappeared directly in front of the young man.

Dominus' features were deeply cut with the creases of anger as he blocked the young man's path to the room. His sudden appearance startled the young man, "How did you do that?"

Dominus looked the young man in the eye, refusing to yield. His voice was calm, controlled, but stern, "I will not be ignored, boy. Get out of my home. You sleep with the animals tonight. When I have decided you are once again worthy of a bed, you will be allowed to return."

The young man raised his hands to push Dominus out of the way, but held short. He stared into Dominus' face for a few moments, "Fine. I will sleep in the barn."

He turned sharply away and walked slowly to the cabin door. He hesitated momentarily before unbolting the door.

He was giving Dominus a chance to change his mind, but Dominus said nothing. The young man looked over his shoulder towards the bedroom, but Dominus was not there. He quickly looked over the other shoulder and saw Dominus sitting back in his chair puffing on his pipe in front of the fire.

Dominus didn't look up or give him any further consideration. The young man snorted under his breath as he opened the door and walked to the barn.

Chapter 3

The young man woke to the sounds of birds and beams of sunlight peeking through the cracks in the barn walls. He hadn't slept much as he was constantly awaken by the strange noises and sounds of the forest that had filled the night. He stretched lazily and allowed the pleasantness of the morning to flush his senses.

He chuckled half-heartedly at the thought of the previous night's confrontation with Dominus. He didn't know how he was going to get through to the old man, but he was certain he was not going to put up with his relentless domineering much longer.

That thought had barely entered his mind when a deep, loud screech broke his silent reflection. It was immediately followed by the squealing of a pig in distress. The young man rolled to the edge of the loft and looked through the door towards the paddock that contained the pig.

The pig was in the grasp of great claws as it rose swiftly off the ground. The young man quickly climbed down and ran to the door. He looked skyward and saw a huge winged creature flying west with the pig in its talons.

He quickly thought, "What kind of creature is big enough and strong enough to carry off what is easily a seven hundred pound pig?"

Watching the creature disappear in the distance, a cold bead of sweat trickled down his face.

Dominus came running awkwardly towards him. His voice was clearly distressed, "What is going on? Where is my pig?"

All the young man could do was point to the sky in the direction the great beast had flown. Dominus followed the young man's finger and was immediately angry, "You let it take my pig? What were you doing, boy? Why didn't you stop it?"

Dominus swung his cane hard around and made contact with the side of the young man's knee. The young man winced in pain and fell to the ground. He looked up in disbelief at Dominus standing above him. The cane was now above Dominus' head and was starting a downward arc towards him.

The young man gasped sharply and rolled quickly to his side and scampered to his feet as quickly as he was able. There was no mistaking the shock he wore on his face, "What are you doing, you crazy old man? It's not my fault. That thing was huge. What could I possibly have done to stop it? Besides, I was in the loft. It was long gone before I could get out here."

Dominus' anger remained, "In the loft? Why were you still in the loft? It is late. You should have been up tending to the animals. You should have been in the paddock and turned it away. It probably would not have come if you had been there."

The young man shook his head wildly, "Are you crazy? If I had been in there that thing would probably have carried me off instead of the pig."

Dominus raised the cane again as he walked towards the young man, "What? You think you are more important than my pig? Do you honestly think it would rather carry you off for its meal?

"I doubt it would have had a taste for you. You could have at least tried to do something."

He brought the cane down sharply towards the young man who stepped briskly out of the way. The cane struck the ground harmlessly.

"Dominus, stop it. You are going to hurt someone with that thing."

Dominus' brow was furrowed as deep as it could be, "That is the idea. It will be you, hopefully. This isn't a game, boy. When are you going to realize that I am not playing around here?"

Dominus raised the cane again and brought it swiftly down towards the young man. This time he didn't move. He waited and when the time was right he raised his arm and swung it down to catch the cane in mid flight. In one movement he ripped the cane from the grasp of Dominus and tossed it aside.

"Enough! I'm sorry about your pig, alright? There was nothing I could do about it. I'm sorry." he hesitated for a moment, "I am more than a little worried that that thing will come back and take one of us."

All anger instantly left Dominus' face and was replaced with a smile. As the smile grew he appeared to grow younger. Within seconds Dominus suddenly appeared to be twenty years younger.

The young man was shocked at Dominus' sudden change, "What?"

Dominus turned away from him and picked up his cane. Without a word he started to walk back towards the door of the cabin leaving the young man standing with his jaw hanging open.

A few feet from the door and without turning, Dominus spoke jovially, "Close your mouth, boy. This is a barnyard and there are flies everywhere."

Dominus chuckled loudly. The young man shook his head and yelled after him, "What was that thing anyway?"

Dominus replied, "Soon, boy, soon."

Dominus turned and entered the cabin. The young man stood in silence for a moment before searching the sky once again for any sign of the beast. Satisfied all was clear, he returned to the barn and without even thinking about it, started his morning chores.

After the barn had been set right, he walked back outside to work in the paddock. To his surprise the pig was back and feasting in the trough.

Confusion lit the young man's face as he once again scanned the skies. He knew he had not imagined the beast. He knew he hadn't imagined the pig being carried off. He knew there was only one pig, and this was it. He knew he had the confrontation with Dominus. He knew all these things to be true, yet as he stood here, none of that now seemed to have actually happened.

The young man abruptly tossed aside the

implement in his hands and stormed out of the paddock towards the cabin door. He was determined to get answers.

As he made his way the sky changed from morning into night. The seconds he took to cover the distance seemed to affect the progression of the day. He saw it, recognized it, accepted it and didn't concern himself with it as he advanced. Answers were all he wanted.

The young man burst through the cabin door and stood beside the table. He scanned the room. There was no sign of Dominus anywhere. He stomped to the closed doors of both bedrooms and opened each in turn; nothing. He turned back to the living area and went back outside.

The sun was high in the sky again. Night had seemingly passed and now it was daylight once again. The young man spotted Dominus sitting on a chair in the circle of chairs. He knew Dominus hadn't been sitting there when he had first stormed towards the cabin. That, too, was something the young man ignored as he walked towards him.

The young man's eyes didn't leave Dominus as he proceeded. Suddenly the loud familiar screech of the beast filled the sky.

The young man dropped to one knee and

looked skyward in the direction of the sound. Seeing nothing he returned his attention to where Dominus had been sitting. He was no longer there. The young man stood up as he turned slowly around in a circle and searched for Dominus.

As he turned, the sun again dropped and night came. Within minutes the silence of the day was replaced with all the screams and roars and sounds that had filled his ears that night several days ago, or was that yesterday. He couldn't be sure how many days had passed nor did he care.

He turned around and around searching the perimeter, the horizon, and the sky. He desperately searched for signs of anything.

Confusion, fear, and anger engulfed him. His mind began to spin. Everything he had seen existed then didn't and then did again. He spun around and around, completely out of control. Then he fell to the ground uncontrollably and passed out.

Chapter 4

The morning sun warmed the young man and slowly woke him. As pleasant as it was to wake this way, it was the poke in his ribs that brought him fully awake.

The sun was in his eyes, but he recognized the shape of Dominus standing over him, "Oh, good. You are still alive. Get up, you need to eat."

The young man shook off the effects of his slumber as Dominus walked away. Through squinting eyes he could see the thing Dominus had just stuck him with.

It wasn't the cane he was expecting, but rather a piece of wood carved in the shape of a sword. The old tattered robes Dominus had worn were now fine silk and his appearance was not of a very old man, but rather he now looked like a man in his mid sixties.

The young man shook his head as he stood and followed Dominus. Looking down at himself, he saw that the simple robes he had been wearing were now gone and replaced with loose pants and white jacket held closed with a black fabric belt double-wrapped around his waist.

The old cabin, too, was gone. In front of him was a very well maintain stone building painted in a bright white and covered with a red tiled roof. The paddock and barn no longer existed, either. The young man picked up his pace to catch up with Dominus.

Dominus didn't slow as he entered the house and moved towards the table in the middle of the room. The young man followed and took a seat across from Dominus. A plate of food sat waiting for him.

The young man looked at the food. It was a veritable feast of eggs, bacon, pancakes plus a glass of water and a cup of fresh coffee. The sight of it brought a guarded smile to his face.

He looked at Dominus, "What is going on here? Last I recall you were a very old man in rough robes who lived in an old run-down cabin with a few farm animals. Today, it's nothing at all like that?"

Dominus nodded lightly, "I am not surprised. You have had a very rough couple of days. You took a nasty shot to the head. You have been hallucinating and have been having night terrors. You have been sleep walking, too. I was beginning to wonder if you had gone mad or something." Dominus smiled at that.

The young man examined Dominus' face intently, but could not see any visible falsehood in his expressions. Dominus saw the confusion and doubt on the boy's face, "Forget it, boy. You appear fine now. You haven't eaten in a few days. You must be dehydrated, too. Eat; drink! You can rest this afternoon. Tomorrow we shall return to your training in earnest."

"Training?" That word captured the young man's attention fully. "What training? What kind of training?"

Dominus remained silent for a few moments before he spoke again, "You don't remember? You have been here for some time now. I hope you haven't forgotten everything you have learned.

"You came to me to learn the arts. Literature, language, philosophy, history, mathematics, music, and of course, battle. I have been a master for many years. When you arrived, I was retired. You intrigued me and I decided to come out of retirement to train you."

Dominus paused for a moment before he continued, "Do you not remember? You have been here for months. Is all you have accomplished now gone?"

The young man searched his memory as hard as he could. There was nothing. He remembered the sharp pain on the bottom of his feet that first morning, but there was nothing before that. He finally shook his head, "I remember you waking me by smacking my feet with a big stick. That is the furthest back I can recall. I don't even recall my own name."

Dominus shook his head, "I have never smacked your feet. I will assume that is the day you took the blow to your head and your hallucinations altered the actual events surrounding it. That being the case, let us hope your memory will return to you.

"As for your name, it is the custom to drop your name in training. Your name identifies you as an individual. That in itself is the epitome of selfishness and is counter-productive.

"You are known only as *boy* and that will not change until your training is complete and I give you your new name. The fact you don't remember your name pleases me. It shows me everything up to now has not been wasted."

Dominus shook his head lightly, "Alright, enough of that for now. Eat. I have a few things to do. Will you be alright if I leave you alone for awhile?"

The young man picked up the fork and began eating. He nodded lightly in response, not really sure if he would be or not. As he ate he continually searched his memory for anything before that first morning. Try as he might, he was not able to recall anything; his own name still escaped him. That was the only thing that truly concerned him.

With the meal complete, the boy followed the direction Dominus had gone. As he walked he could hear the sounds of grunts and thumps. His mind identified the sounds as being the result of hand to hand combat.

As he grew closer he could see thirty men and a half dozen instructors working on techniques and methods in a grassy area behind the house. He could also see a long building on the other side of the grassy training ground. He was certain that was the barracks that housed these people.

Further past this field was an area that was separated from the rest by a rock wall. He knew that was the area that was reserved for him and Dominus. He didn't know how he knew, but he knew it was the special place for his individual training.

As he walked along he could see some of the other students hesitate to watch him pass. It was not the curious glance of someone looking at a stranger passing by, but rather a glance of familiarity. The boy didn't think he knew any of them, but it was clear they knew him. Nonetheless he continued past.

Arriving at his training area, the young man could see Dominus working on some of his own moves. The word *forms* came to the boy's mind. Dominus was working on his forms. The young man knew the term was correct, but couldn't remember how he knew.

The young man thought that title a bit odd as soon as it came to him, but the distinction was clear. He couldn't remember anything prior to a few days ago, but he knew there was far more buried within him that he just couldn't remember at this moment.

As he approached, Dominus stopped what he was doing and turned towards him. He spoke compassionately, "What are you doing here? I told you to rest. Did you finish your food?"

The young man nodded politely, "Yes, thank you. It was very tasty."

Dominus laughed, "I'm glad you enjoyed it. It was definitely comfort food. Do not expect meals like that again. From now forward you will return to the usual meals.

"Your meals will be simple and include fruit, rice, fish and water." Dominus chuckled at that, "So why are you here? Do you expect to do some training?"

The young man nodded, "I feel fine. I might as well get back to it, whatever it is."

Dominus hesitated as he scanned him from head to toe, "Very well. You can work on your *forms*, but that is all. No weapons. No sparring. Is that clear?"

The young man nodded, "Thank you."

With that, the boy proceeded through a regime of carefully choreographed stretching methods before starting. There was no conscious thought on his part. He simply went through the motions as if some ingrained instinct was in control.

After several hours, he stopped and sat on a nearby rock. The smile on his face was unmistakable.

Dominus too was smiling as he walked towards him, "It is good to see that you have indeed not forgotten your lessons. It would have been rather unpleasant starting from the beginning again."

Dominus nodded affirmation, "That is enough for today. Tomorrow we can start back with earnest. I am convinced that you are none the worse for wear.

"Our first task will be to correct the problem that caused that head injury in the first place. Clearly your defense needs a bit of work."

The young man chuckled lightly, "That sounds good to me." He rose from the rock and headed down the path towards the front door of the stone house. Once inside, he proceeded directly to the food pot in the kitchen area and filled a bowl with food and began eating before he had reached the table.

Dominus arrived after him and took his own bowl of food and sat at the table across from the young man, "After you eat, you should clean up and turn in. A good night's rest will do you a world of good."

Without looking up from his dinner the boy nodded agreement.

Chapter 5

The morning came far too soon for the young man's liking. His room was ideally situated in the house to catch the first rays of the morning sun. In general, it is a pleasant way to wake and start the day, but today he would rather have slept in. He stretched out into the most comfortable position under the blanket and granted himself a few extra minutes sleep.

Eventually, he knew he must rise. His neatly folded clothes sat on the chair near the bed where he had left them the night before. It had become his practice to neatly pile his clothes on the chair before retiring. He smiled as he dressed and walked into the main area of the house.

Dominus was already at the table having his breakfast, "Good morning boy. I trust you slept well?"

The young man smiled and nodded, "Yes, I slept very well but it was difficult getting up this morning. The bed was far too comfortable."

Dominus nodded knowingly, "That would explain the lateness of your rising. No worries. I allowed it today. Once you are fed and watered we will head out to the training grounds. I'm sure you will feel less like resting and more like working when we get there."

The young man smiled as he retrieved a bowl of food. As he sat, Dominus spoke again, "Today we shall continue where we had left off. Do you recall where we were?"

"No, I do not." The young man shook his head, "I still don't recall anything before that first morning I told you about yesterday."

Dominus nodded, "Not to worry, I am certain your memory will return eventually. Either that or you are in for one nasty beating, again." Dominus chuckled as he rose from the table and headed out the door.

The young man smiled and finished his meal. When he was finished he headed out of the house and up to the training grounds. Dominus was busy in his warm-up, but stopped when the young man entered the enclosure.

"I hope you are well fed, boy, but not too full to work."

The young man smiled, "I wanted more, but I thought better of it. I am ready."

Dominus laughed, "Very well. We'll start with a little hand to hand. I wouldn't want to open your skull if you have forgotten all you have learned."

The young man smiled gratefully. Dominus approached the young man as he was starting his own stretches and warm-up. Dominus smiled, "You slept in, you don't have time to nimble up. Game on." With that, Dominus threw a left kick towards the young man's head.

The young man immediately came out of a warm-up stance and into an aggressive defensive stance. As he blocked the incoming leg with his arms, he kicked his leg towards Dominus' mid section. Dominus laughed openly as he blocked the young man's foot and tossed him on his back all in one move.

The young man looked up at Dominus standing over him. Dominus smiled, "Good. It is clear you have remembered. You are rusty, but you are reacting well. Now stand and work through your warm-ups. I am satisfied we can proceed."

The young man smiled as he picked himself off the ground, "I am glad you are pleased, but you dropped me far too easily."

Dominus nodded, "Of course. Do not worry. The time will come when that will no longer be possible for me to do. I am as certain of that as I am about the ground beneath my feet." The young man smiled and returned to his warm-ups.

Hours turned into days. Then days turned into weeks and weeks turned into months. The training continued undisturbed. Whether rain or shine or snow or any other test nature could throw at them, they trained and they studied.

One day after a particularly hard practice session, Dominus called the young man to his side, "You have learned well, boy. I am not easily impressed, but you have impressed me. There is little else I can teach you. You are ready to move on."

The young man smiled with pride, "Thank you. It has been a real honor to study under you. You have taught me a great deal. Far more than I could have ever expected."

Dominus nodded and was about to speak again when something thirty feet from them caught his attention. Dominus lost all expression as he turned to face the presence.

The young man turned with a start in the direction Dominus faced.

A creature like nothing the young man had ever seen before walked towards them. It was adorned in a fine flowing cape. The cape was black on the outside and blood red on the inside. Beneath the cape the form was dressed in a finely tailored black suit. What flesh was exposed from beneath the garments was blacker than night and completely void of any visible hair. It moved so fluidly one would think it was flying.

As it drew closer, the young man could see the hideousness of its features. Its face was the deepest black. The boy thought of looking into a deep, deep hole and the blackness of those depths would be embarrassed by the blackness of this creature, yet its features appeared almost human. Its K9 teeth were long and yellow stained. The rest of the teeth in its mouth were pointed as any flesh eating animal's would be. Its eyes seemed to glow with redness surrounding the deepest black pupils. Looking into those eyes gave the young man the feeling of peering into death itself. It was as unnatural a look as any he could recall ever seeing. The beast's fingers were long and bony with long nails protruding from their tips. The nails were stained black and looked more like claws than nails. Imagination would suggest perhaps the stains were from the fallen victims of this creature.

It ceased its motion five feet in front of Dominus but its attention was fixed on the young man. Dominus spoke sharply, "What do you want Abaddon? You know you are not welcome here. You agreed to never come here."

Abaddon remained fixed on the young

man for a few more seconds before casually bringing his attention to Dominus. It was then that the young man noticed how tall this Abaddon thing was. It easily stood two full feet taller than both Dominus and himself and easily double their combined width. It was an imposing presence to say the least. But even at that, the young man did not fear what he saw.

Facing Dominus, Abaddon spoke with a voice deep and dark, "I heard you had a new apprentice. I had to see him for myself. Is this feeble little thing him?"

Dominus didn't flinch. He simply chuckled lightly, "Oh Abaddon, you will never change, will you? Yes this is my new boy. He is a strong one and really quite brilliant."

Abaddon laughed and as he did saliva dripped from his fangs. When his laughter stopped he looked towards the young man, "This boy is familiar to me. I have seen him before. Last I saw of him he was a pathetic little thing. Hardly something I would consider brilliant or strong. So what is this *mighty warrior's* name? Or is he permitted to have one?"

Dominus smiled, "The boy has a name. I have given him back his own name. He shall continue to be known to all as Zane. Zane Wilder."

Abaddon snapped his head back toward Dominus with surprise, "Really? You must think very highly of this young one to give him his own name back. For your sake I hope he lives up to expectations."

Dominus' voice was calm and smooth, "I can assure you he is very capable. I have no doubt of it."

Abaddon laughed again, "Well, he is going to have to be."

Dominus' voice didn't waiver, "I am not concerned, nor is he. You and yours will not continue to harass the innocents."

Abaddon turned again towards Zane and scanned him from top to bottom, "We shall see."

Abaddon turned sharply around and retreated in precisely the same direction he had come.

Zane turned to Dominus, "Zane? Really? My name is Zane. Zane Wilder. I like it."

Dominus looked at Zane and smiled pleasantly, "Consider yourself very fortunate. I rarely give anyone their original name back."

Zane was stunned and involuntarily stepped back. The voice, the mannerism, all of it, was precisely as he remembered Dominus in his *hallucinations*. Zane was about to speak again when Dominus pointed off to the left and spoke sharply, "Look lively, Zane. One comes to test you. Let there be no mistake, this is not a game. This is not a sparring match. This will be a fight to the death. There is no second place."

Zane was still confused by Dominus' change in mannerisms. As he spun in the direction Dominus pointed he saw another black beast identical in appearance to Abaddon. It was approaching swiftly. This one wasn't wearing clothing. Even without clothes its gender was indiscernible. Every muscle in its body rippled as it moved. Its frame was as gorgeous as a fine work of art, but its face and claws were hideous. It mattered little at this point. It was clear that its intent was battle and it was equally clear it had no intention of being defeated.

Zane was not prepared and was still a little confused. He hadn't had time to prepare for a fight. He was tired from the full day of training he had just finished and his mind was already focused on a meal and rest.

When the beast was ten feet from Zane it slowed. The great black wings on its back spread wide and it spoke with a gargled voice, "You are about to die little one. Make your piece with your God. You will soon be nothing more than a meal."

It folded its wings back and leapt towards Zane. Zane reacted more from his trained instincts than anything else. He dove forward towards the beast, but under its flight path and tumbled through a front roll and returned to his feet behind the direction the beast had gone. He spun around quickly and prepared himself.

Zane pulled his Gladius from its sheath at his side and stared at the beast. It leapt towards Zane again. This time Zane stepped slightly to the side as he swung his short Gladius in an arc and struck the beast in the ribs as it sailed by. The creature screamed violently from the pain and rolled to the ground, but rose quickly. Zane watched in horror as the wound he had just inflicted began to heal before his very eyes.

The rage on the creature's face was unmistakable. Drool dripped from its fangs and it emitted a low growl as it focused and prepared for its next attack. Zane didn't move. He remained calm and focused. He did allow a small smile to warm his face and watched as the anger in the beast grew at the sight of it.

The low growl turned to a blood-freezing roar as the beast attacked again. This time Zane waited patiently as the creature approached. At precisely the right moment he thrust forward as hard as he was able and watched as his sword drove half its length into the mid-section of the beast. It roared from the pain, but managed to swing its arm across its body, striking Zane squarely on the side of his head. The blow was powerful and it sent Zane through the air and tumbling on the ground. He recovered quickly and rolled to his feet. He once again faced the beast, but now he was unarmed. He shook his head as if to try and clear it. Still hurting from the blow, he knew he didn't have the time to dwell on it. There would be time to heal later.

The beast tipped its head backwards and roared in a mix of anger and pain as it pulled Zane's sword from its body. For a moment it was still as it looked at its own blood coating the blade. It then looked towards Zane as it tossed the Gladius aside. Its expression changed slightly. Zane decided it was this creature's way of displaying an arrogant smile.

It moved slowly and deliberately towards Zane. Its arms were positioned in front of it and slightly bent at the elbows. It hunched forward to what was clearly an attack posture.

Zane watched its approach and laughed tauntingly. The sound of the laughter infuriated the beast even further and it quickened its pace Zane glanced in the direction of his sword. It wasn't too far away. All he needed was to find a way to get to it.

The arms of the beast came closer together with the intention of taking Zane around the throat. Just before it made contact with him, Zane shot both his arms in an arc in front and away from his body forcing the beast's arms apart and then with both fists together, Zane punched hard into its torso where his blade had entered. The creature's blood still marked the wound and made the target easy for Zane to find.

The wound was already starting to heal, but was not healed fully and the beast roared from the force and the pain. Zane kept his hands together as he ducked under the beasts arm and swung his own arms in an arc and struck the area of the cut in the beast's ribs. It roared again in agony. With one more arc, Zane drove both fists into the back of its neck just below its skull and it dropped to its knees.

Zane knew this was sufficient a distraction and he raced towards his blade. The beast recovered quicker than expected and leapt at Zane with its hand outstretched. It grabbed Zane just above the ankle. Zane landed hard, face first into the ground. With a grunt, Zane reached his hand out as far as he could and was just able to grasp the hilt of his sword. As he got a firmer hold of it, he could feel himself being pulled backwards.

With the sword now firmly in his grasp, Zane rolled to his back and sat up with the sword swinging in a loop down towards the arm that was holding him. In one swift motion the beast's hand and lower arm separated from the rest of its arm at the elbow. The roar it made this time was almost deafening.

Zane scrambled quickly to his feet and shook his leg to break the grip of the creatures severed limb before it had a chance to tighten up. It fell limp into the dirt as the beast stood slowly. It looked at the wound where its lower arm and hand had been. Then it looked down at the ground at its hand and lower arm laying in a pool of blood. It charged towards Zane in a boiling rage.

Zane held his ground as the creature approached. When the time was exactly right, Zane stepped to the side where the creature's arm had been significantly shortened. Zane swung his sword confidently with the back of the creature's neck as his target.

The beast realized the intent of the incoming blow and adjusted its course enough to avoid the blade. It tumbled deliberately to the ground and with its good arm grabbed its severed arm by the wrist as it continued to roll back up to its feet.

It stood and faced the surprised Zane. In its

hand was its own severed arm. It took the arm and mated the two cut ends together and held that position for a few seconds. When it released the grip it had on its own wrist, the severed arm fell to the ground. It was clear to Zane that the beast had expected the arm to reattach. The thought of a creature having such an ability was unnerving to him and the whole proceeding had momentarily rendered Zane incapable of moving.

The beast looked down at its arm in the dirt before reaching down and picking it up again. When its focus returned to Zane, it was much calmer in its movements but the rage was still on its face. Blood dripped slowly from the stub attached to its shoulder but the wound appeared to be healing over. The wound on its chest had closed. It was still visible, but was no longer bleeding. The wound Zane had created on its ribs was now gone.

Zane saw the work he had done and shook his head at how the beast was able to heal itself so quickly. He realized without doubt that the only way to win was to remove the beast's head from its body and not allow it to put the two back together.

Before Zane had a chance to formulate a plan, the beast started towards him, slowly. It held its own arm in its grip as a club. Although Zane had been trained to expect the unexpected and be always prepared for the unexpected, the sight of this surprised him. This absolute disregard for its own body was not something any amount of training could have prepared him for.

At seeing Zane's surprise, the beast took the opportunity to advance its attack. It raised its severed arm above its head and swung it down with a speed Zane didn't expect. The still wet end of the arm connected squarely with Zane's jaw. Thankfully the meat that was still on the bone cushioned the blow somewhat, but it was still sufficient to knock Zane to the ground.

Zane rolled in an effort to diffuse some of the force of the blow. On the ground he quickly rolled further from the beast and stood. Now standing, he refocused on the beast. He had allowed it an advantage that thankfully he had been able to survive. That was something he could not afford to do again.

Zane loosened his grip slightly on his Gladius. Not too much, but enough that the tensed muscles in his arm wouldn't slow the speed of his arm. Facing the beast he slowly side-stepped while remaining face on. With each step he slowly moved closer to his adversary.

The beast kept pace with Zane, never giving him an advantage. It spoke in voice that sounded wet and slurred, "Zane Wilder, today is not your day. I will enjoy beating you to death with the limbs I rip from your body."

It laughed heartily and cautiously closed the gap between them. Both combatants carefully tried to move to a position of advantage and each failing. Finally Zane let out a loud battle cry and faked a lunge towards the beast.

It responded immediately by lunging towards Zane. Zane smiled in anticipation and leapt as high as he could as he swung his sword in a smooth arch that connected with the back of the beast's neck. The sword only hesitated slightly on the vertebrae as it passed through. The creatures head tumbled to the ground with the rest of the body following close behind.

Zane moved forward quickly and kicked the head further from the torso. He then stood over the body with his sword at the ready for a few moments before he was satisfied it was indeed dead. He then turned towards Dominus. Dominus was smiling and looking toward the spot where Abaddon had been.

Zane spun sharply to look in the same direction. Abaddon smiled and nodded towards Zane, "Nicely done, Zane Wilder. You have learned well."

Abaddon turned and walked slowly away. His voice boomed as he departed, "We will meet again Wilder."

Zane remained fixed until Abaddon disappeared from sight. He then wiped his blade on the grass before turning back towards his fallen adversary. To his surprise the body of the beast was gone. He snapped his head towards Dominus but only caught a sight of him walking down the path towards the house.

Zane followed after him. As he walked, he noticed the training green and all its students were gone. The barracks was also gone. The white washed house was gone. All were replaced once again with the old log cabin, paddock and barn.

Zane stopped in his tracks and looked all around the area that surrounded him. All his memories from the time of his 'hallucinations' came back to him. He was again completely confused. Is this reality and the place he had just been was the illusion or is this the hallucination that has returned? Perhaps the battle had caused a relapse.

"Yes", he thought. "That must be it. This is the illusion."

He continued towards the front door of the cabin fully expecting it all to change back at any moment. It didn't and he forcefully walked through the door of the cabin. At the table sat Dominus. He was now younger than he had been only a few moments ago. Now he appeared to be a man in his forties.

Zane shook his head and reached for his sword, but there was nothing there. He looked down to the place where the sword had been and saw his complete attire had returned to the robes he recalled wearing during his "hallucination".

Zane looked sharply at Dominus, "All right, enough. What is going on here? I want answers? I think I deserve answers?"

Dominus didn't speak. He simply pointed to the table and the full plate of food that sat upon it. He turned and ignited each candle and the fireplace by pointing at each, then returned his gaze to Zane.

Zane hadn't moved. Dominus smiled. His voice was calm and almost nurturing, "Please. Sit Zane. Eat. I have much to tell you, but first you must eat. You will need your strength."

Zane remained standing and looking at Dominus. Dominus gestured again towards the food. This time Zane acknowledged the gesture and sat at the table.

He looked Dominus in the eye, "First things

first. What was that thing? Where did it come from?"

Dominus sighed, "First thing? No, that is definitely not the first thing. I have much to tell you, but that is definitely not the first thing."

Zane smiled, "So that wasn't an illusion. So this place then, this is an illusion? Yet here I sit. So are both places an illusion and reality is still some other place?"

Dominus smiled, "Yes, and no. All your questions will be answered in good time, Zane. Eat first, and then I will tell you everything you need to know."

Chapter 6

Zane looked at the plate of food in front of him and then back up to Dominus, "Eat, eat. What is with you and eating? I am not hungry. I don't want to eat. Tell me what is going on."

Dominus nodded and smiled, "That is good. Hunger is something you will never feel again. In fact, you have never actually felt it since you arrived here. You have simply eaten because it was within you to do so. It was simply something you felt you had to do without knowing why. I told you to eat and you ate. Now you accept that that isn't necessary."

Zane shook his head, "Make sense already. No more games. No more riddles."

Dominus nodded, "Very well. Let's sit by the fire and get more comfortable."

Dominus didn't wait for acknowledgment as he rose from the table and sat in his usual chair. He immediately began preparing his pipe. A pint of ale appeared on the table next to him.

Zane watched for a moment then rose and sat in the chair next to him. He stared at Dominus for a few moments before he spoke, "Well?"

"Have a little patience, my boy, patience.

Look at the fire. It is so peaceful."

Zane turned his attention to the flames and watched the orange, yellow and blue flames dance to the melody of their own creation and was quickly mesmerized.

It was then that Dominus broke the silence, "Do you still remember the first day you were here?"

Zane looked at Dominus, "Yes. Why?"

Dominus nodded and spoke calmly, "Continue to watch the fire."

Zane returned his attention to the flames. A few moments later Dominus spoke again, "Try to remember before that day. Think hard. Stare at the fire. Concentrate on the fire. It will clear your mind and allow you to look deeper into yourself."

Zane's tension began to slowly wane. The flames continued their dance. The orange and yellow colors began to shrink and the blue became more prominent. He continued to watch the flames as faces appeared within the flames, one after the other. All appearing and vanishing far too quickly for him to recognize any of them. He tried hard to identify what it was he was seeing. More and more scenes and faces flashed through the flames. The speed at which they appeared began to slow and he started to identify who and what it was he was seeing. "This is me. These are the people and places I have known."

The scenes continued passing through the flames and Zane was totally engrossed. He didn't dare blink. As he continued to focus, scenes began coming in clumps. Most of what he was seeing he recognized as scenes from his past. Some of the scenes he didn't recognize but assumed that they, too, belonged to his life. Those were undoubtedly events he had forgotten for one reason or other.

Time passed and he remained totally focused. The scenes sped up to an incoherent stream of color and movement and suddenly the fire popped loudly into a single flame of pure white. The white flame remained momentarily then gave way to the more expected dance of the colors of a normal fire.

Zane slumped back in his chair and was breathing heavily. Dominus didn't look up from the flames, but nodded with satisfaction. When Zane caught his breath he turned to Dominus, "That was my life wasn't it? That was a display of everything that I have ever done and everyone I have ever known. It was my entire life summed up and displayed within the flames?"

Dominus nodded.

Zane shook his head, "Why? Why are the

images and memories in the flames?"

Dominus responded instantly. His voice was matter-of-fact, "Because you are dead."

Zane's jaw dropped, "Excuse me? I'm dead? What are you talking about? I am as alive as you. I sit; I eat; I drink; I breathe; I bleed."

Dominus chuckled, "Well, actually, that is not entirely true. The images in the fire were indeed from your life. It was a life that you left some time ago.

"Every person, place, and thing you knew in your life was displayed there in the flames. None of it exists now. Well at least not in the black and white context of life and death that you are familiar with.

"The human mortals that you were once among will now be known to you as *Liberi;* children. You are no longer one of them. You now exist in a place and manner far different than anything you could possibly imagine. Your life as Liberi is gone."

Dominus could see the confusion on Zane's face and he chuckled. "In the context of the *Liberi,* I am more than twenty three hundred years old. In the context of true time and space, I am ageless."

With that Dominus changed again and appeared much younger. He now appeared to have the same physical age as Zane, a man in his early twenties.

"I was a legionnaire for Rome. I was a skilled warrior. I died in battle. When I arrived here I was as confused as you are now. Perhaps I was even more confused than you are now. I came from a time in Liberi history with far greater ignorance of the realities of existence than you. When I arrived, I was taught much as you have been taught. My teacher has long since moved on."

Zane grew angry, "So all this time I have had no memory what-so-ever of my past. Now you show me my whole life just so you can tell me that it doesn't exist?" Zane shook his head in disgust, and spoke sarcastically, "Thank you so much!"

Dominus was about to speak, but Zane spoke again, "So then, what is this place? Is it heaven or is it hell? My vote is hell."

Dominus shook his head, "Neither. There is no heaven or hell. They are concepts created for religious purposes for the sake of Liberi. They are concepts shared by a great many other young civilizations throughout the universes. Believe me, I had the same questions in my day."

Dominus paused for a moment before continuing, "Religion was adopted by the Liberi a very long time ago. It has been modified and altered as needed to fit their respective environments, cultures and peoples. It has always been essential for the Liberi to have religion. The race is simply too immature to exist without it.

"There has always been just enough fact interlaced within it to keep it believable and useful. As time passes for the Liberi, the need for religion as they have known it will also pass. Their beliefs will be augmented and/or replaced with a great knowledge beyond your wildest imagination."

Dominus took a draw from his pipe, savoured it, and then exhaled slowly. That was followed by a mouthful from his tankard. He paused momentarily to appreciate both before continuing, "My pipe and my beer are two of the luxuries I allow myself. I have no need of either except for the simple pleasure they provide. The realities of these pleasures, too, do not actually exist, but I make them exist for my own purpose."

Dominus took another draw from his pipe, "The Liberi would certainly destroy itself if some rules and codes of conduct were not created. The whole concept of right and wrong needed to be created. The creation of those concepts needed to be based on something greater than Liberi. Civilization itself could never have occurred without some common doctrine to hang onto. It really is as simple as that."

Dominus nodded lightly before continuing, "I am going to assume you recall your lessons on the structure of the universe. What you need to realize is that the universe you have known is not all there is. There are a great many universes on a great many planes and dimensions.

"Picture in your mind all the galaxies in the Liberi universe. The distance between each is massively huge.

"Now imagine another universe, if you can. Imagine that universe intersecting the Liberi universe. It could do so without actually touching anything within their universe."

"Now imagine the Liberi's own galaxy, the Milky Way. It is a mass of stars and planets all held together in one plane of existence by gravity.

"Within this one galaxy, the distance between stars is huge. In fact, another galaxy, Andromeda, will pass through the Milky Way a few billion Liberi years from now. Not one star or planet within that galaxy will touch any planet or star within the Milky Way. However, the gravitation influences of both will forever change the shape and characteristics of each. Everything that had existed in each galaxy will continue to exist, only in a different way."

"This example is exactly the same as the intersection of universes only with universes it is on a much larger scale. A nearly infinite scale. All these universes, and there are more than I even know, intersect each other, some within the same plane of existence, others not."

"The hardest thing to grasp is the fact that it is possible for beings to transfer between universes and planes at the point of those intersections.

"You and I are in one of those intersections. Actually every planet in every universe is connected to a great many other universes through this same way."

"It all probably seems complicated and unbelievable to you. Simply understand this one thing, it is possible for you to travel immense distances as easily as crossing the street by way of these intersections.

"It is also important for you to understand that it is just as easy for other species to travel this way as well. Abbadon and his race are doing exactly that.

"Time is also an interesting concept. Everything in your past and in the existence of the Liberi has a finite beginning and a finite end. One is born, lives and dies. All things progress in a linear fashion along a hard course of time.

"Nothing could be farther from the truth in reality. Time and space are as pliable as a rubber band and can be manipulated and altered to any shape or use."

Dominus smiled with the pleasure of sharing the information he had learned over the millennia.

Zane shook his head not yet understanding what he was supposed to be learning, "What does all that have to do with me? How does that explain why I am here? How does it explain all that I have been through?" Zane hesitated a moment before continuing, "Millions of people die every day. Why am I the only one here? It just doesn't make any sense."

Dominus nodded acceptance that his explanations to Zane may be flawed or to complex for him to understand at this point. The simple realities of existence are exceedingly difficult to explain when the student has limited understanding and background.

Dominus took a few moments to think and to try to find the words to explain things better, "You are correct in saying that millions die every day. In fact the number is far greater than either of us can even imagine.

"You are the only one here, because I chose you to be here. My last student finished and moved on. I had a vacancy and you became available, so I took you. It is that simple.

"But in as simple as that is, I did have many to choose from. I chose you for very specific reasons. Reasons you don't really need to know or understand. Just know you were chosen and leave it at that."

Dominus chuckled, "When a creature dies, it is only the physical being that ceases to exist, the essence continues.

"Some return to the place they left and are reborn. Some remain unseen within the same environment they had lived before dying.

"Sometimes, if the conditions are just right, those that live in that environment can occasionally see those that have died. In rare occasions, some can even converse.

"Others move onto other places within the universes. Much of this is plain chance. Some of it is time and place coincidence. A very select few are chosen for a specific purpose, like you.

"The essence of you had the characteristics I require in the pupils I choose to teach. When I finish with them, they move on to another place to continue their existence until it is time for them to once again move on." Dominus paused for a moment, "I didn't know where you would be going when you left here until I saw Abaddon. He is one of the creatures that only targets the Liberi. The Liberi don't know they are prey because of us and many others like us.

"He is an outcast from a very long time ago. He and his cohorts find pleasure in hunting Liberi. It is because of his appearance here today that I know you will be living amongst the Liberi."

Dominus paused again for more smoke and drink before continuing, "I am but one of a great many teachers. There are a great many pupils in training at any given time and in a great many places. All are being prepared for an existence somewhere else. You are by no means unique, but you are definitely amongst a select group. Relatively speaking."

Zane shook his head, "So what exactly am I supposed to do?"

Dominus smiled, "Like I said earlier, creatures from all over the universes find their way to existences in other places in the universes. Some find their way to the Liberi. Some of those are of no threat to Liberi. Those individuals live amongst the Liberi in peace. There are others who have the intention of hunting and feasting on Liberi."

Zane repeated himself, "So what is it I am supposed to do?"

Dominus smiled proudly, "For lack of a better term, you are a babysitter or perhaps policeman if you prefer. You will live amongst the Liberi and you will protect them from the harm that could come. You will protect them from themselves and from others. Believe me, you will be busy."

Zane's voice was quiet, "So creatures like that one earlier are going to be coming and I will have to fight them?"

Dominus shook his head, "No. Not fight them; kill them. Fighting implies the chance of losing. Losing is not an option. Like your battle today, there is no second place. If you fail, you and a great many Liberi will die."

Zane nodded solemnly, "Will they all look like that creature today?"

Dominus shook his head, "Those creatures are known as vampires to the Liberi. Most of the tales of the vampire have evolved and changed with time."

Dominus chuckled, "The Liberi have made these vial, blood thirsty savages almost romantic in their stories. That in itself amazes even me. To answer your question, no. You will see a great many species that you will consider exotic and some you will consider weird. They will not all be like Abaddon and his kind.

"There are a great many different types of beings that you will need to deal with. Some will never let the Liberi actually see them, while others take joy in allowing themselves to be seen just prior to the kill.

"Like most things, they have the ability to phase in and out of planes and therefore visibility. And before you ask, look deep into the memories that you have. Think of the stories you heard as you were growing up. Think of all the myths, the legends, the fairy tales and the horror stories.

"Most of the creatures in those stories are real in one form or another. They have been altered in the stories by imagination, but they are all based on reality."

Zane was growing a little prouder, "If they are phase shifting, how will I find them before they phase into visibility?"

Dominus nodded, "You will have no trouble seeing them. You will remain in the natural form of the Liberi. You will appear as you did when you were in that existence.

"However, you will be out of phase with them. You will be able to see them and everything they do, but they will not see you.

"You do, however, have the same ability to phase from your plane into theirs. This is a tool you will find useful, but it is also a tool you must use wisely."

Dominus paused again as he tapped out the charred remains in his pipe in to the ash tray beside him, "That is enough for now. Sleep. We will resume again tomorrow."

Zane chuckled, "Sleep, really? I thought sleep, like food, would be something we no longer require?"

Dominus nodded with satisfaction, "Alright, you are getting it. That is good, Zane Wilder."

He paused briefly before continuing. He then pointed to the door, "Outside there are things that you must deal with. They will determine once and for all if my decisions and choices were wise.

"You have already known of them from earlier in your lessons, but you will soon know more of what they are. You will remain outside until the sun rises. If you are still alive in the morning, you will be ready to move on. But be warned, you will need to call on all you have learned to ensure you see the light of day again. Fare well, Zane Wilder. Fare well."

Zane nodded, rose and without another word walked out into the dark.

Chapter 7

Zane walked deliberately to the familiar circle of chairs and sat down. The darkness was as calm and quiet as he could ever remember. There wasn't a sound above the grass rustling in the breeze. Zane was sure he could even hear the fire crackling behind him inside the cabin. He jumped with a start when Dominus arrived beside him. "I didn't hear you coming."

Dominus looked down at him in the chair and barked, "You cannot sit in that chair. Sit over there. There are plenty of chairs over there."

Zane was a little shocked but got up and moved without hesitation. Dominus sat in the chair next to the chair Zane had just been sitting in.

Zane looked at him then at the now empty chair, "So what is the big deal about that chair?"

Dominus remained quiet for a few moments before finally looking at Zane. The expression on his face was solemn, "I told you I was killed in battle a long time ago. What I didn't tell you was that I was a newlywed.

"My wife and I had been married for less than a month when I had to march. I shouldn't have been gone more than a year. It didn't work out that way."

He paused and tried to shake off the emotion that was welling up within him. "I have been waiting for her to join me ever since. For more than two thousand years I have been waiting for her. I believe one day she will find herself in a plane that will bring her back to me. No one sits in her chair, no one."

Zane nodded sympathetically. He understood without understanding and he didn't press the topic further. There wasn't much else to say. Love for a woman is the most totally encompassing thing a man can ever face. It can give him great strength or drive him to his knees. Zane knew that Dominus hadn't been with her long enough for that dedication to wane or tarnish as familiarity can sometimes do. He felt proud of him and he pitied him too.

A sharp, high pitched squeal broke the silence. It was the sound he had heard before in the dark, and the sound he had heard when the pig had been taken. It made the hair on the back of his neck stand up. He scanned the skies hurriedly but could not see where the sound originated.

As he cast his eyes about, sounds from the forest began to grow louder and louder. It was reaching a crescendo of cacophony that seemed intent on making him insane. He refused to yield and allowed every sound of every pitch to reach him. He made a conscious effort to sort the mass of sounds into their individual parts. Closing his eyes assisted to that end, but it was a state he knew he dare not maintain.

With a calm flowing over him, he was able to once again open his eyes and scan his surroundings. All was as it had been. Nothing had moved. The orchestra of noise had been successfully sorted into a logical manuscript of sounds and the confusion of his senses waned.

With focus he was able to discern the classes of sound. Some were human, some were undeniably animal, but some he didn't believe to be either. He looked over at Dominus sitting stoically in silence. There were no clues from him.

Zane returned his focus to the forest line to search for any sign of movement. Suddenly, out of the corner of his eye, he caught a glimpse of something moving. He quickly turned his entire focus towards it.

Out of the darkness, a medieval knight on his mount, with lance poised, rushed towards them. Zane leapt to his feet and moved to intercept. Raising his hands together, a long shafted spear appeared in his grasp.

He looked at the implement with a knowing smile, but quickly returned his focus to the foe approaching. His brow lowered as he focused. His stance altered for the best position. Zane's timing was exactly right as he knocked the knight's lance off its course and forced his spear to penetrate the knight's armor.

As soon as the tip of the spear was set on its way, Zane let go and dove away from the attack. The lance and the end of the spear both missed him as the steed continued past, but there was no mistake that the spear had found its home in the ribs of his attacker. A few feet past, the horseman fell to the ground and lay motionless.

Satisfied, Zane returned to his chair and proudly looked towards Dominus. Dominus' face was completely void of emotion. He didn't acknowledge Zane in anyway. It was as though he had not seen what had just transpired.

Zane was about to speak when another sound caught his attention. He spun around and focused on the forest. Out of the wood walked a wide array of creatures. All of the faces and creatures he recognized from the memories Dominus had made him relive.

Zane thought, "How? How is this possible?"

He stood up again and walked around to face the approaching mob. As they moved, some turned and walked back into the forest, while others kept coming. With each step forward, more turned away and walked back into the forest, until there were only a handful of beings in the clearing facing him. None approached any closer than a few dozen yards, but Zane recognized them from the illustrations in stories he had been told as a child. The renderings he recalled paled in comparison to the sight of the real thing before him.

They were evil looking beasts and their presence in tangible form sent shivers down his spine. They stood staring at Zane without making a sound. It was as if they were waiting for him to make some move or to say something. He didn't. He simply stood his ground and regarded them in the same stern silence they offered him.

After what seemed an eternity, the last of them turned and headed back towards the forest. As they went, Zane could hear them laugh. As they broached the edge of the forest one spoke, "We will meet again."

With that the air was again calm and quiet. All that could be heard was the rustle of the breeze in the grass. Zane nodded proudly and returned to sit in his chair across from Dominus.

The first light of dawn began brightening their surroundings. Dominus raised his head and eyes to focus on Zane, "Dawn is breaking and you are still alive. Congratulations."

Dominus paused for a moment, "So, Zane, do you have any idea what happened?"

Zane nodded with pride, "I have been judged. The essence of those I have known have given their vote. Only one challenged my ability. Several others reserved their judgment for another time. But it is clear that I am ready to move forward from here; whatever forward from here means."

Dominus nodded, "Indeed. You will fare well in your next existence, of that I am certain. I shall miss you. Not more than the others that came before you and no more than the ones that will come after you, but I will miss you nonetheless."

Dominus paused for a moment then spoke again, "Search your mind, Zane Wilder. Do you see what is there now?"

Zane concentrated deeply, and then his eyes went wide in amazement and he shot back further into his chair. All he could say was, "My God."

Dominus stood slowly, "I have given you your final lessons. What you have just seen were the words and images that language cannot covey.

"All the accumulated knowledge of the

Liberi is now within you, as is much of the knowledge of existence. Use it wisely, Zane Wilder."

Without saying another word Dominus made his way back to the cabin. As the door closed behind him, the barn, paddock and the other out-buildings slowly began to vanish. Within moments there was nothing in the clearing but Zane. He stood up, and as he did, the chair, too, vanished.

Seconds later the high pitched squeal was heard again. Zane raised his hand and a broad sword appeared within it. He nervously scanned the skies and forest that surrounded him. Moments later the air was disturbed by the sound of great wings. Out of the sky to the east, Zane saw for the first time the full view of the creature that had carried the pig away.

Zane took a defensive stance as the great beast drew closer, wrapping both hands firmly around the sword and raising it to an attack position. However, to Zane's surprise the creature landed twenty feet away from him. The shape of its head, the fork of its tongue, and the breadth of its wings all told Zane that he was in the presence of a great dragon.

Zane knew he was either to be prey, or master. After carefully weighing what he had learned, he was prepared to take the risk that the second option was the correct one and he tossed the sword aside. It vanished before it hit the ground. The dragon's eyes followed the course of the sword until it disappeared then returned its attention to Zane.

Zane took a deep breath and began to slowly walk towards the dragon. The great beast watched him carefully as he drew nearer. When Zane was inches away, he reached out his hand to its snout. At first it pulled away, but quickly lowered its face within reach.

Zane smiled as he gently stroked the soft, scaly flesh, "You and I are to be companions apparently. Well at least until I get to wherever it is I am going. I hope you know the way as I have no clue."

The dragon snorted and swung his head to point at its back. Zane understood immediately and climbed up and grabbed hold of whatever he could. He was no sooner in place, than the dragon leapt into the sky and flew off to the East.

Chapter 8

Riding on the dragon's back, Zane flew towards the dawn for what seemed an endless amount of time. The sun seemed to just hang stationary in one place without rising any further. The ground below was obscured by a heavy mist. Zane had no idea where they were. He was relying completely on the dragon for guidance and trusted it knew their final destination and how to get there.

Eventually, trees, valleys, oceans, meadows and cities appeared in front of them. They looked quite far distant and small, but grew quickly as they approached. The speed they were travelling was far greater than Zane had imagined.

In minutes, they landed on a grassy area in a park. The trees in the park appeared to be unnaturally spaced and obviously manually placed. A baseball diamond took up one corner of the park with a children's playground in another. Cars and a parking lot sat between the two. The children near-by played and his arrival appeared to have gone unnoticed. Families were everywhere enjoying the pleasantness of the day and this place. Although he knew without question that he had never been here before, the surroundings were familiar, and he took comfort in that.

He smiled as he dismounted the dragon. A small child ran headlong towards him. Zane flinched instinctively, but he realized he wouldn't be able to get out of the way fast enough. No matter, however, as the child simply went through him as if he wasn't there. Zane looked down at his own body with surprise. Zane seemed completely intact, and he hadn't felt a thing as the child passed through him.

Zane looked around the near vicinity as he smiled with a hint of amusement. It didn't appear anyone had noticed the arrival of the two of them. This surprised him further. "How could one not notice a dragon and rider sweeping in from the sky and landing only feet away? One wouldn't think such a thing would be commonplace enough to be ignored."

There was no denying however, that they had indeed arrived completely unseen. Seconds passed before a couple more boys came running towards them laughing. Again, both simply ran through Zane and the dragon.

This time one of the boys slowed and turned to face the direction of Zane. There was a definite puzzlement on his face, but it passed quickly and he resumed his course to catch up with the other boy.

Zane looked at the dragon for a hint, but it

seemed unconcerned. It was as though this was something it had experienced before. Zane shook his head, as he reached up and patted his winged steed on the neck, "It would appear you know what is going on. Glad one of us does. I wish you could speak and tell me what you know."

The dragon returned Zane's gaze as though it understood what he was saying and was frustrated at not being able to answer the question. Zane chuckled lightly at the sight of it before returning his attention to the people and vistas that surrounded them.

It was then that Zane noticed a young man in his mid twenties leaning against a tree with his arms folded across his chest. The young man wore a sinister smile and appeared to be looking directly at Zane and his ride. His dress is of the same style as the Liberi that were scattered about the park and his long brown hair was swept by the breeze.

The dragon noticed the man too. When he did, he let out a deep but pleasant roar as he rushed towards the tree. Zane yelled after him, "Stop, dragon, stop!"

It completely ignored Zane as it continued toward the tree. The man stood away from the tree and put his right hand out in front of him. The dragon ground to a halt and bowed his head towards the man's hand.

The man was patting his head as Zane arrived, "Sorry about that. I don't know what got into him. How is it you can see us? No one else around here seems to be able to?"

The man didn't divert his attention from the beast for a few moments and when he did he stared into Zane's eyes, "You are one of Dominus' aren't you?"

Zane was puzzled, "Dominus? Yes. Why?"

The man laughed from his belly, "Good ol' Dominus. You might want to rethink your attire. Not much call for Roman tunics here." The man shook his head before continuing, "What name has he given you?"

Zane was puzzled, "Zane. Zane Wilder."

"Alright Zane, Zane Wilder, walk with me." The man waved his arm casually to some unknown place in the distance.

Zane nodded agreement reluctantly, but walked with this individual. As he walked he willed a change of clothes that more closely matched the few Liberi he has seen so far. The dragon lay down in the grass as if it knew it wouldn't be needed.

The two had walked for several minutes before the man finally started talking, "I have been known by a good many names in my time, but for you, you can call me Ducis." Ducis chuckled lightly. "Or if you prefer, you can call me *sir*."

Zane stopped and turned towards Ducis, "Sir? I don't think so. You are the same age as me, hardly someone I would call *sir*."

Ducis smiled and his voice was almost jovial, "I appear to be the same age as you, but believe me, I am far older than you. But that is a story for another time and another place. Never mind the sir; Ducis will be fine." Ducis chuckled lightly as he started walking again.

Zane wasn't amused. His expression turned to one of impatience bordering on anger. Ducis saw it and smiled, "Sorry. I haven't had anyone new to work with in quite some time. I have been looking forward to your arrival. Not you specifically, just someone new."

Questions flooded Zane's mind, but he held back, deciding that Ducis would provide the information as Dominus had. At the same time, Zane hoped Ducis would be a little more forthcoming with far fewer riddles than Dominus.

The two made their way to the fence line of the very well maintained ball park and stood facing the diamond. They both enjoyed the pristine view in silence.

Ducis finally broke the silence, "We don't

exist in the same plane in this universe as the Liberi occupy. However, we have the advantage from our plane to interact with their plane.

"I am not really sure how, but it really doesn't matter beyond the simple fact that we can. That is probably the best way to describe it. They cannot see us, or hear us, but we can see, hear and even touch them.

"Our presence can be felt by some of the more sensitive ones, but they are few and far between. Most of them usually dismiss us as a draft or some such thing. We've even been referred to as ghosts by some. That is rather amusing if you think about it."

Ducis chuckled lightly and shook his head before continuing, "I have even heard of instances where a Liberi, being tired or in an unusual state of mind, caught a glimpse of us out of the corner of their eye. It is an interesting tidbit, but not really of any importance or consequence."

Zane was startled by the bluntness with which Ducis had broken the silence, "Nothing like letting me in gently. I have about seven thousand questions now."

Ducis laughed, "Yes. I imagine you do. I will tell you all you need to know. The rest of the answers will become apparent soon enough. Grant me some patience and it will save us both a lot of time."

Ducis paused to gather his thoughts before continuing, "First of all, I think I would like to talk about us and why we are here. That is as good a place to start as any I think."

He paused again momentarily. When he began, his voice was rich and proud, "We have to exist somewhere. We have been chosen to be here. We exist on this world and amongst the Liberi. We conduct ourselves within the realities of our existence and theirs. We simply exist as ordinarily as they do.

"It is also important to note that there are far more of them here than there are of us. Most of us just mind our own business and carry on our lives as we see fit. You will learn how to spot our kind amongst them soon enough."

Ducis continued, "Ordinarily the Liberi can't see us, however, if circumstances dictate, we can make ourselves visible to them. You had better have a very good reason to make yourself visible to them.

"It has been done in the past many times and usually the results are less than desirable. Entire religions have been created because of our appearance. Just take a wander around this area and you will see half a dozen religious facilities within a few blocks of where we are standing now. That is not a coincidence."

Ducis paused a moment before continuing, "There are others, however, which I will talk about later, that still do it. Their motives are far from sincere. Most of them aren't like us. Everything about them is different. They look different and have different values and beliefs. We are more of a nuisance to them in some ways and in other ways we are a very real threat."

Ducis smiled and nodded as if acknowledging his belief of what he had just said, "As you go about your time here you will hear many strange things, but you will know exactly what they are referring to. Most of their legends, myths, horror stories, fables and the like are really their own interpretations to explain us and the others. Some of them are dead wrong, but some are not.

"You have the ability to talk to the Liberi any time you like. They cannot hear you the same as you and I are talking now. We have the ability to make suggestions directly into their minds and they will perceive them as their own thoughts. What they hear is what they call, 'a little voice'.

"They have their own thoughts and weigh those against their little voice within their own intelligence. Our voice works with their consciousness and appears to them as a conflict within their own mind. It can be useful at times. Again, not something you want to play with. Ensure you have good reason."

Ducis chuckled, "As brilliant as the Liberi think they are, they really aren't too bright. We could appear in front of them with all the accumulated knowledge of mankind, tell them exactly what they need to do and they will do the exact opposite. It seems that their attitude is almost out of spite.

"Our indirect methods of speaking to them through themselves gives the illusion that it was their idea all along. Some of us are here, and other places like it around the world. We are along the 33rd parallel. That is 33° N latitude on this planet.

"This parallel is the entry point from a great many planes and universes to this one. Not every kilometer of this parallel can be accessed from other planes, but there are many entry points.

"Some of the new arrivals stay here, but many venture off to other places or cities around the world. I don't mean to imply that they are all evil or vicious. Some are little more than tourists from other places, but all of them need to be watched. There are a great number of us all over the world to keep watch."

Ducis gathered his thoughts, "Along with us doing what we do, there are other groups of us who deal with the most intelligent Liberi on the planet. Their job is to ensure the Liberi don't get too far ahead of themselves.

"The Liberi have the ability to create technology way beyond what they are currently using, but they do not have the maturity to use it wisely. So many of us make sure they progress at a pace realistic to their maturity.

"There have been some amazing geniuses in the history of the Liberi, but they were only able to deliver their ideas and knowledge once we permitted it."

Zane was about to speak but Ducis shut him down, "Later. Let me finish. We have plenty of time. Don't worry."

Zane conceded and adjusted his seating. Ducis continued, "It is also important to note that our physical strength is many times greater than the Liberi. Why that is necessary or how that came to be, I am not sure, but it is a reality.

"Many of us were Liberi before coming here so I am not really sure where the added strength came from. I don't really care either. It is simply one of those things to note.

"As well as the knowledge we possess. I'm

not really sure how that was made to happen either. Dominus knows, of course, as do the other teachers. I just know that all of a sudden it was all there."

Ducis pointed his thumb over his shoulder in the direction of the dragon, "He will be leaving shortly. His purpose has been fulfilled and you won't have further need of him. Dominus assigns a dragon, usually this one, *Larspike*, to all of his pupils when they depart.

"It is intended to be a ceremonial transition from Dominus' training to this place. In reality, it isn't necessary but it does give the new ones the sense of leaving one place and arriving at another. Why a dragon you might ask? Frankly, that is just Dominus' sense of humor and irony. That's it."

Ducis hesitated and his expression became far more sombre, "The Liberi have no clue that there are far more universes than just one. It is also important to know that not all Liberi come here when they *die*. It is also critical to know that not all the creatures you will encounter were Liberi."

Ducis paused to allow that information to sink in. After adequate time he continued, "Through the history of the Liberi there are tales of powerful monsters, creatures that thirst for blood, creatures that hunt the Liberi and there are also creatures that aid the Liberi.

"We are amongst the latter. You will encounter the others in your travels. You will not have difficulty spotting them and their desires will also be obvious. Let there be no mistake, Wilder, they will try to kill you. You will have to fight them. You will have to fight for your very existence. If you fail you will leave this place and move on to the next one.

"None of us know what that is. It could be a better place, or it could be a far worse one, none of us have any idea where it will be. But more importantly, you will leave the Liberi vulnerable to the whim of the others.

"You will undoubtedly come across names like Vampire, Werewolf, Sasquatch, Yeti, Gargoyle, Boogy monster and on and on. Those are the creatures of legend and myth and they are the ones that you will have to be wary of.

"They must be terminated on sight. This I cannot stress enough. I'm sure Dominus has already told you that. In fact I am sure of it. I would like to tell it to you a hundred more times just to get it across to you. It is that important to your very survival and to the survival of the Liberi."

Zane raised his hand and a long spear instantly appeared in his grip, "I am ready for whatever comes along." Just as quickly the spear vanished.

Ducis chuckled. It was not a pleasant tone, "Ah, the vanity of innocence and ignorance. You have no idea how powerful some of these beings are. Do not underestimate their abilities. I know you wouldn't be here if Dominus didn't believe you are ready, but don't underestimate the others. You don't get a second chance."

Zane smiled, "I have already fought one of Abbadon's pets and clearly I won. I feel I have the ability to fight whatever I need to, whenever I need to."

Ducis smiled, "Dominus is one of the best. I have no doubt you have been very well trained. However, in all battles the mind is your single strongest weapon. Use it well and you will be victorious. Be foolish and *you will* perish."

Zane smiled again, "So I will hear all those names for the others, but what name do the Liberi use to describe us?"

Ducis nodded lightly, "Yes, they do have names for us too. We have been called Angels by some, Gods by others, or ghosts, or demons, or witches and warlocks. Some have even called *us* monsters.

"For our purposes it really doesn't matter what they call us. Our purpose is what it is and we will simply exist and do what has to be done. If our paths should cross that of the others, we will never hesitate to do what must be done."

Zane stood in silence for a few moments. Then he began walking slowly through the baseball diamond in deep thought. He needed time to process all he had been told. Ducis didn't move. He knew Zane would need some time. He chuckled to himself as he watched Zane walking without yielding to the Liberi.

A ball game had begun while they talked. Zane walked his path, even if it took him right through a Liberi. It was clear to Ducis that Zane had at least grasped some of what he had been told.

Eventually Zane was just a speck on the horizon. Ducis decided enough time had passed. He ported himself to Zane's location. Ducis appeared, seated on a bench only a few feet away from Zane. The sudden appearance of Ducis startled Zane, "Geez, man, what are you trying to do? Kill me."

Zane realized what he said and laughed openly. Ducis simply smiled, "You will get used to it, don't worry."

Ducis continued, "You still have many questions. Is there anything you would like to know right now?"

Zane looked thoughtfully towards Ducis, "Frankly, I don't know what to think. I am here obviously. It is also obvious I was somewhere else a short time ago. I may fight for my very existence with creatures that I can only imagine. No one asked me if this was something I wanted to do. Just suddenly here I am. I'm not sure I want to be here."

Ducis nodded, "It is like that with most new arrivals. When you were born as a Liberi, you grew into being a Liberi and learned as you went.

"Here, you don't have that luxury. Here, you have to hit the ground running and you have to be educated and capable from the very beginning. No small task, I know.

"If it is any consolation, I will be here to help you adjust. You won't be alone. I will be like a, hmmmm, trainer, or handler if you will."

Zane shook his head, "If you are here, why do I need to be here? Surely there is somewhere else for me to go. There must be other places. Otherwise this place would be over-run with others like us."

Ducis chuckled, "There are a great many places in this world. As I have already told you, this is where you belong. You will learn and you will live and you will learn to live. That is all."

Ducis frowned, "There are a great many beings in an infinite number of levels of existence and dimensions. Many of the others come here to simply live. For them it is merely a new and beautiful place. Some come here to hunt. Not all, but many.

"The Liberi are merely another form of game to them. We protect the Liberi from those creatures when the need arises. We don't have to do it. It isn't our doctrine or anything. Well, I guess it is our doctrine in the strict sense. It is a primary purpose.

"Everything else we do is will, but protecting Liberi is what we are primarily here to do. It is simply the way it has always been and it is the way it will always be. At least until such time as they don't need us any longer. The others don't value the life of the Liberi as we do."

Zane stood silently for a few moments. When he spoke again his voice was sullen, "How do they get here?"

Ducis nodded thoughtfully, "They get here the same way you and I got here."

Zane shook his head, "How did we get here?"

Ducis chuckled, "I haven't got the foggiest

idea. Apparently that is one thing you and I don't need to know. Understandably so, I guess. We'd probably go elsewhere if we could so, it is probably best that we don't know how that is accomplished, but obviously others have learned how."

Zane was not satisfied with the answers but knew that was all he would be getting from Ducis, "How will I know which ones I have to fight and which ones to leave alone? How will I be able to defeat them? What if I can't defeat them?"

Ducis sighed knowingly, "You may well not be able to defeat them. There have been many before you that have failed. There will be more after you.

"You have been given all the tools you need. The only true variable is your own will. Believe you will win and more than half the battle will already be won. Believe it."

Zane spoke softly, "How long will I be here?"

Ducis looked away for a moment before returning his attention to Zane, "This is your new reality. You will be here until you leave. You are no longer a Liberi. Here there is no deadline. There is no life expectancy. You will not grow old and die in your bed. Mortality in that sense does not exist here. Time in that sense doesn't exist for us. You will learn to understand that too."

Zane took a deep breath, "It is conceivable then that I could be here for eternity?"

Ducis smiled. It wasn't pleasant. "It is conceivable, but highly unlikely."

Zane questioned Ducis' expression, "So you don't hold much faith in my survival? That is certainly comforting. And whose decision is it anyway, whether I stay or go?"

There was definite sincerity in Ducis's voice, "That's not what I meant. I always hope the newbies last forever. It has been my experience, however, that none do. If I were to guess, I would say none were ever intended to be here forever. I have even witnessed some simply disappearing right before my eyes.

"I believe it was their time to move on and that was that. As for who makes that decision, frankly, I have no idea. I don't know that anyone or anything consciously makes that decision. Perhaps there is a consciousness out there in charge of such things. I simply don't know.

"I know there are a great many things in the entire envelope of existence that I don't understand. I have learned to accept that and do the best I can with the knowledge I have. That is really all any of us can do.

"I have been here for thousands of Liberi years, many thousands of years. I have no idea when I am to leave or how that will happen. Frankly, it doesn't matter really. I like what I do and will continue to do it for as long as I am here."

Zane nodded in contemplation. After a moment he began walking again. He was headed back towards where he had left Larspike.

Ducis walked with him, "Do you have any more questions for me?"

Zane shook his head slowly. Without looking at Ducis he spoke but his voice was barely a whispered, "Not at the moment."

The two continued in silence back to Larspike. When they arrived, Larspike was nowhere to be seen. After scanning the close proximity, Zane looked to Ducis and with a sigh, "Him too?"

Ducis smiled sympathetically, "As I said, his job is done. He got you here. He has more than likely gone back to where you came from. Where ever that may be. He may be back here someday, but I can't guarantee anything."

Zane nodded slowly as he continued his scans, "So now what? What am I supposed to do now?"

Ducis' mood improved suddenly, "Anything you want. You are free to wander about and check things out. You can find a place to call home. You are not required to be anywhere. This is your life now. Live it. Learn your way around. You can do whatever you want to do."

Zane didn't try to hide his confusion, "Seriously? That's it? I arrive in this place where no one can see me. I am free to do whatever I wish. I have no purpose aside from what you have told me. So what, am I to sit on a bench until I am needed to fight or whatever?"

Ducis responded instantly, "No. That is not at all what you are to do. I think you need a little more time to figure things out. Why don't you go and wander around town for a while. Get a feel for the land and the places and the people. Meet me back here when the sun rises again and we can talk some more. It really isn't as doom and gloom as you are making it sound. Really it isn't.

"Oh, and one more thing. It is not a small thing and it is quite rare, but sometimes the power we possess gets the best of us. Some start to abuse the powers they have been given. Like I said, this is rare, but it does occur. If you notice any of us acting in a manner that is contrary to the best interest of the Liberi, it will be your responsibility to, ummmm, terminate them."

Zane nodded lightly and started off towards a part of the park that appeared to be attracting the greatest number of people. Zane appeared completely unaffected by the words Ducis had just spoken.

When he was well out of range, Ducis looked skyward, "Are you sure about this one? He seems far too unsure of himself. I am thinking that perhaps he shouldn't be here or at least not left alone."

A voice responded in Ducis' head, "I am sure. If you recall, you weren't much different when you first came here."

Ducis sighed as he nodded his head, "Very well then."

The voice spoke again, "So why do you still hide your real name? All of that was a very long time ago."

Ducis nodded, "I know, but I am still not very pleased with the way I handled things or myself back then. None of us are. It is best to leave the slate clean. That is all."

"I know, but it was also because of those times that much of what we now do and believe came into being. That history was not all bad. And why tell him to kill on sight? Do you not think you deserved a second chance?"

Ducis simply chuckled as he walked towards the east and vanished from sight.

Chapter 9

Zane found a bench with a good view overlooking the playground where children played and laughed. He couldn't help but smile. He sat quietly and enjoyed their innocence. It gave his mind a calm that allowed him to contemplate everything that had transpired and to try to figure out how he was to fit into his new existence.

He sat alone on the bench for quite some time. A while had past when a rather large woman came along and sat in exactly the same place Zane was occupying. Her presence in this spot had no effect on him other than making him uneasy.

He looked to the back of her head as he spoke softly, "I think it is far more comfortable to sit on one of the ends of the bench rather than right in the middle."

The woman casually looked to either end of the bench. Once she had decided which end of the bench looked better, she rose and moved over. Zane smiled with relief and satisfaction.

The woman no sooner sat back down, when that end of the bench tipped hard sideways. The woman rolled off the end of the bench onto the ground. With her weight now off the bench it crashed down to its original position. Clearly the anchors that were normally in place to prevent such things from happening were missing.

There was a loud outburst of laughter from those in close proximity that had witnessed the woman's distress. Zane chuckled as well before a twinge of guilt took hold. He knew none of this would have happened had he not suggested she move.

He quickly moved to the woman to try and assist her to her feet. He reached down with his hand, but it passed right through her. He shook his head. He had forgotten that he was still unable to directly interact with Liberi.

A young man who had also witnessed the accident came rushing over and offered the woman his hand. She looked up at his smile and was angry, "What is so funny, young man? Is it good sport to see a fat woman fall off the bench?"

The young man continued to smile, "You have to admit, ma'am, it is pretty funny. It would be just as funny if it happened to me or anyone else for that matter. Slap-stick comedy, that is all. It has nothing to do with you personally."

The woman paused before she too started smiling, "I suppose you are right. It is pretty funny. I probably would have laughed too. That is after I was sure the victim was okay."

The smile eased on the young man's face, "Right. Sorry. Are you alright?"

The woman smiled and reached her hand up to his, "I am fine. Thank you very much for coming over and helping me. It is a very considerate thing for you to do."

The young man's smile returned. By then a couple other people had arrived and all offered a form of assistance to help her regain her feet. One of the others chuckled, "I am glad you are okay, but man, I wish I had got that on video."

Everyone laughed. The woman nodded gratitude, "Thanks everyone. I think I will be calling the city and suggesting they do something to fix this bench."

She sat again, but she returned to a spot on the middle of the bench. The helpers that had come to her aid wandered off to resume their activities. Zane looked at the woman on the bench and wanted to apologize, but knew that whatever he said at this point was mute.

Instead he smiled and walked to a more secluded spot and sat on the grass under a tree. It, too, was a good location for watching the fun on the playground. His smile returned and he remained in the same spot, without moving, for the rest of the day.

The sun passed high overhead and started to drop towards the west. The light of day slowly gave way to the beauty of dusk. The majority of people had now left the park to continue their day elsewhere. Zane remained seated on the grass until long after the sun had set.

Finally he rose and started walking slowly towards what he assumed was the downtown. It was time to do a little exploring. He didn't have any particular place to go and was in no hurry to get there and his pace reflected that. Hours passed as he walked up this street and down that street. He paid attention to everything he passed and committed as much as possible to memory.

Several hours later, he found himself walking through a parking lot at the back of the Owl and Gate pub.

Fifty feet away he could see a group of men. As he grew closer he could tell that they were engaged in a fight. A few feet closer he realized it wasn't a fight so much as a beating.

A man on the ground was using his arms as a shield in an attempt to ward off the blows the three men over him were delivering. Zane rushed in to assist. He reached his hand out to the first rather large man he came to, but as in the park, his hand passed right through.

Zane shook his head angrily before he looked to the back of the man's head, "Alright. He's had enough. I think he got the message."

Almost instantly the large man stopped his attack and reached his hands out to his two friends and stopped them, "He's done. That's enough. Let's go."

The three turned away from their victim and quickly headed off in the opposite direction of the pub. Zane quickly knelt beside the man on the ground and examined him as best he could.

He had sustained some very serious looking injuries and was in grave distress. His head was covered in open wounds that were bleeding profusely. He was curled in a fetal position, clearly guarding internal injuries. His clothing was soiled and torn. His breathing was shallow and raspy.

Zane rose and looked around as a police cruiser stopped in a spot adjacent to the pub. Zane stared at the officer behind the wheel and spoke towards him, "Check the parking lot. Check the parking lot."

The officer gathered himself as he spoke into the car radio, and exited the cruiser. He looked quickly at the parking lot and then started to make his way in the direction of the pub. Three steps later he stopped again and looked into the parking lot. He changed course and started walking towards Zane and the fallen man.

As he grew closer it became apparent that he had finally seen the man on the ground. His pace quickened significantly as he made his way to the two of them. As he moved, Zane could hear him calling for assistance and an ambulance into the microphone clipped to his collar.

He knelt on the ground beside the victim and surveyed his injuries, "It's alright sir. An ambulance is on the way. You will be fine." The officer attended to what injuries he was able to in anticipation of the ambulances arrival.

Zane was satisfied that he had done all he could do. He slowly started off again to resume his walk around town.

Suddenly a realization came to him. The images of the three men flashed in his mind. He felt the rush of blood leaving his body. He recognized them, "Those were the men that killed me. How is that possible? Why would Dominus allow people from my past to be here?"

Zane raced off in the direction the men had gone. He searched everywhere in the area, but there was no sign of them, "They must have a car and driven off." Zane's brow furrowed and his voice deepened with anger, "I will find them."

Zane now wanted dawn to arrive quickly. He needed some answers. Zane impatiently made his way back to the park to meet up with Ducis.

Chapter 10

By the time Zane had reached the park the sun was already up. He had taken a roundabout route to get to the park in hopes of seeing the three men again. He was unsuccessful which only helped his resolve grow.

Ducis was seated on a bench overlooking the children's playground. At this time of day there is no one there, but even so, it is a pleasant place to sit. Once Zane reached Ducis, he sat and looked at him silently.

Ducis smiled as he turned to Zane, "So, how was your first day? Are you getting used to it all yet?"

Zane didn't return the smile and his tone was controlled, "I just saw the men that killed me. Why would Dominus put me here knowing I would run into them at some point? I want to know what is going on. I want to know everything!"

The surprise on Ducis' face was unmistakable. His brow dropped and the wrinkles of worry of a far older man framed his deep green eyes. He snapped his attention skyward, "Dominus? Is this true? Are there Liberi here from his past?"

The questions were met with silence.

Ducis tried again, "Dominus! I demand you speak to me."

Finally the voice of Dominus boomed, "You aren't questioning my judgment are you? I have reasons for all things."

This time Zane spoke, "Why are there Liberi from my past here? How many of them are there? Why here? This wasn't my home."

Ducis snapped his attention to Zane, "You can hear Dominus?" Then he snapped his head skyward again, and yelled, "He can hear you? No one ever hears you but me. I think you need to explain what is going on!"

There was silence for a few very long moments before Dominus spoke again, "Yes, Zane, you have been returned to the approximate time you left. Most of the Liberi you knew in your life still live, but none of them remember you.

"Do you recall the fire in the cabin that night? The one where you saw all the faces and places from your past. Do you recall the forest's edge, all the people and creatures from your life?

"Well, that was not simply a stroll down memory lane. It was the process of them being called up and you being erased from their minds. To them now, you were never born. You never existed."

Zane spoke angrily, "What? Why? The only thing I have that is truly my own are those few memories of my life. Now everything I recall never happened?"

Dominus spoke sharply, "To you, everything that happened was real. Everything you recall *did* happen. However, to everyone you knew, none of it happened.

"I have my reasons. I have my reasons for putting you back in the time you left. I have my reasons for their memories of you to be erased. I have my reasons for bringing you and requiring you to remain at this entry point on the 33rd parallel. I have reasons for everything I do.

"Telling you what those reasons are would only hinder you rather than help you. Your purpose here is far beyond that of Ducis or any of the others for that matter. I have chosen you for something far greater than you could possibly understand. Yet.

"Everything you have been told about why you are here is true. That *is* why you are here. That is all you need to know. Remember your lessons. There are no accidents. There are no coincidences. Everything that exists has a purpose and every action is for a reason. That is all you need to know.

As for you Ducis, obviously yes, Zane can hear me too."

Ducis was going to say something, but thought better of it. He simply said, "Alright then. So why do you need me to be here for him? If he is to be on some special mission, what possible good am I to him."

Dominus chuckled, "For this one, your work is done. There will be more, but your time with Zane is over. From here on any communications with Zane will come directly from me. Is that clear, Ducis? Do you know what I am saying?"

Ducis simply nodded. He rose from the bench and faced Zane with his right hand outstretched, "It would seem that our paths split here. It was a pleasure meeting you and I wish you all the best. Dominus is a pain, but he is fair. Heed him and you will do well."

Zane smiled, "It really isn't that big a place. I'm sure we will run into each other again."

Ducis returned the smile, "I doubt it. Dominus just told me that I will be moving on elsewhere. This place is now yours."

Zane nodded pleasantly as Ducis turned and started walking. A few yards away he vanished from view.

Zane looked skyward again, "So, Dominus, now what? What is this great plan you have for me? Will you enlighten me as to why the only person I know here has now been sent away?"

The questions were met with silence. Zane looked puzzled, "Dominus?"

There was still no response. Zane yelled, "Dominus, are you there?"

Zane waited for a response, but there was none. Giving up he stood and started walking.

As Zane passed a tree he reached his hand out, and touched it. It was solid and his hand rested against it. Looking behind him, he had felt the grass as he walked, but neither the grass, nor the sand in the playground showed any sign of his passage. Zane nodded his head in uncertain acceptance and continued out of the park and further back into town.

A few hours passed and he found himself in another park close to downtown. It appeared to be a lunch place for downtown workers. As he walked through the park he noticed four people eating at a picnic table.

Zane approached them and tried to touch the closest person on the shoulder. As usual, his hand passed right through. He nodded his expectation. Then he reached his hand down and touched the picnic table. It was solid to his touch, just as the bench and tree had been.

On the table in front of the man was a glass of soda. Zane chuckled and reached his hand to it. After all, if he could feel the trees and the ground and the table, he should be able to feel the cup. He wrapped his hand around the cup and it felt solid. He lifted it to his face and took a drink.

The shock on the faces of those at the table amused Zane as he poured the liquid into his mouth. He could feel the fluid and he could taste it too, but the interesting thing he noticed was the liquid appeared to the Liberi to pour out of the seemingly unsupported raised cup, and vanish in thin air. Zane replaced the cup on the table. As it touched the table the four Liberi hurriedly got up and ran off.

Zane chuckled, "Okay. Note to self, don't do that again." He chuckled and walked towards a bench nearby. He sat and smiled. He knew asking why he could make physical contact with some things and not others would go unanswered.

Even so, he still wondered how it was possible to be in one plane for some things and not others. It didn't make sense. There must be a reason that escaped him, but it really didn't matter. It was his new reality and as in any reality, one learns their limitations within it.

However, now he knew what he could interact with and what he couldn't. That unto itself was useful. Later, in a more secluded spot, he would try to physically move to the Liberi's plane. He assumed that if he were on their plane he would be able to experience all things as they do. He didn't know for sure, but it seemed a reasonable assumption.

The only thing he wasn't sure about was exactly how, he would be able to make that change. He remembered how badly he wanted to be in their physical world. Both the large woman in the park and the man in the parking lot needed assistance, but he had been unable to help.

He wasn't sure what he would have to do to make the change happen. The thoughts had no sooner cleared his mind than Dominus spoke, "You have been having a bit of fun I see, Zane?"

Zane smiled but didn't look up, "Not so much fun. More a matter of determining what it is I can and cannot do."

There was a pause before Dominus spoke again, "You are able to do far more than you now know. Most of those lessons will come with time. You are curious how you would be able to move from this plane to theirs? It is easy actually, but there isn't really a good reason for doing it, so again, I will not tell you how it is done. What you will need to do can be done from your present existence. There is no need to go to theirs. You have already witnessed that. It may not be at a level you would like, but it is at the only level you will need. That is all."

Zane shook his head, "That is not acceptable, Dominus. I could have helped that guy in the alley. I could have dealt with the men that killed me."

Dominus spoke again, "You did help the man in the alley, did you not? As for those men, they looked like the men you knew. This is not your town. Are you sure it was them?

"Do not get preoccupied with your past life, Zane. There is nothing there for you anymore. Wrap your mind, heart, and will around your current existence."

Zane shook his head, "No. Dominus, I don't accept that. There is no doubt in my mind that they were the same guys. I know it with every fiber of my being. I don't know how or why they are here, but it was most definitely them."

There was only silence. Zane waited for a response for several moments, but none came. He shook his head, "Dominus, I don't know your game, but it is clear you are up to something. I will figure it out, of that you can be sure."

Zane headed further into town. It's clear this place was where he was going to be for a while. He thought it best to become familiar with the area. He knew it was on or very near the 33rd parallel, but he did not know this town's name and he wanted to know that. If this was to be his new life and this was to be his new home, he should at least find out its name.

Zane remembered seeing the local Chamber of Commerce and Visitor Center on Main Street. He was certain that whatever information he wanted could be found there. He thought he should be able to simply walk through the door when a Liberi did and have a look around.

As he followed the same route as last night he passed the churches again. This time he noticed the Presbyterian Church. The sign in front said Sunnyville.

Zane smiled, "Well that is certainly a pleasant enough name for a town. I wonder if these people have any idea what goes on around them every minute of every day." He chuckled lightly, "I truly doubt that they do. If they did, most of them wouldn't continue living here."

It took far less time to reach the Visitor Center than he thought it would. As luck would have it, someone was just entering when he arrived and he was able to walk through the doorway with him.

In the lobby a large selection of pamphlets were neatly displayed. Many of them contained information on the surrounding area, and a few had information about the town. He gathered up a selection of local pamphlets, area pamphlets and a map. Zane was very careful to ensure no one saw him as he slipped them into his clothes.

He knew the Liberi would notice the pamphlets floating through the air, but none would notice them once they were neatly stowed inside his clothes. This, too, was an anomaly he didn't quite understand, but the example with the soda in the park made it clear.

Satisfied with his collection, Zane stood by the door and waited for someone to either exit or enter. He didn't have to wait long before he was once again on the sidewalk outside the building. He needed a secluded spot to review the materials he had just gathered.

Next to the building was a parking lot and a paint store. Behind that was a small wooded area that would suffice. He wouldn't be there long and there were still several hours until the sun would be setting.

He made his way quickly. When he arrived

amongst the trees he scanned the surroundings to ensure that he indeed would have the privacy he needed for the next while. Satisfied, he removed the pamphlets and the map from under his shirt and laid them on the ground carefully.

The first item he looked at was the map. Getting his bearings and learning the lay of the land is definitely something he needed to know.

The map wasn't open long before he realized that this little town was only about thirty minutes by car from his home town on the Atlantic coast. He shook his head. He hadn't known this town was here.

All the years he lived thirty minutes away and he didn't recognize the name of this little town. Perhaps that lack of memory was also part of Dominus' plan. He shook his head again. It was folly to second guess Dominus and to look for a motive behind everything.

Further inspection of the map was simply to recall areas he knew and to determine if there were any other places he had been forced to conveniently forget.

A National Forest to the east was not far away. He did recall that forest from his life. It was a truly fabulous area and he remembered many good times in those woods. He wondered quickly if that was the area where Dominus had conducted his training. He shook his head. There was no way to know that for sure and it was doubtful Dominus would tell him one way or the other.

There was also a large lake west of the National Forest. He remembered going there in his life as well. As he reviewed the map he concluded that the route he would have taken to the lake didn't pass through Sunnyville. It is entirely possible that he had not actually been through this town before.

In the same area that together comprised Sunnyville, his home town, the forest and the lake, there was also several military facilities. He remembered those, too. He had never been to any of them, but he did recall them being there.

He wondered quickly if the 33rd parallel was a reason for those bases to be located as they are. He chuckled to himself, "How is that for a conspiracy theory."

Many memories from his life were triggered as he continued inspecting the map. He smiled as he recalled those years. The smile didn't last as he also recalled that everyone that had been a part of those memories no longer knew of him. To them, none of those things ever included him. He wanted to be angry but just couldn't. More than ever he wanted to believe that Dominus had a very good reason for all of this.

Zane looked back at the collection of pamphlets and ignored the ones concerning the area. He knew all that information already. Instead, he pulled forward the information on the town of Sunnyville.

The history of the town wasn't too spectacular. It is a town that has existed for nearly three hundred years.

Many of the buildings around town have the character of the old south. Many people came here in the early days to escape the seasonal bugs back home.

The climate, soil and vegetation are noted for creating an atmosphere that is very beneficial to Liberi suffering from certain lung ailments.

It was all and all, a small town of forty-three thousand people, with all the character and charm only achievable in a small, well established town.

Even the pine trees in this town are protected. It is a town in which Zane now felt very comfortable. It is even a town he would like to live, or rather accept this existence in. Perhaps, he would have liked living here when he was Liberi, too.

He was satisfied with the level of

superficial information he now possessed. He knew the more subtle information would only come with time and experience in the area.

He took a quick look around to ensure no one was near-by before he gathered up all the papers. He would keep the map which would have value many times over, but the rest could be disposed of. A receptacle for such a purpose was close by and he made his way to it.

He had spent more time than he thought in his review and reminiscences. The sun was now beginning to set. He walked slowly back out to Main Street and watched the shadows grow across the ground. Traffic had diminished significantly and it was turning into a very pleasant time of day.

Zane walked back up Main Street in the direction of the Visitor Center. As he passed the glass doorway he looked at it fully expecting to see his own reflection and was taken aback momentarily by its absence.

He chuckled lightly and reached his hand out towards the door. Instead of striking its hard surface, his hand went right through.

The lack of resistance the door offered surprised him, and he turned to fully face it. Taking a deep breath he walked forward. He expected to crash into the door, but instead he walked right through it. He shook his head with uncertainty, not really sure what to think.

Turning and stepping back towards the door, he attempted to tap his knuckles on the mouldings that surrounded the door frame. Again, his hand went right through. He shook his head in confusion

He walked back out the door and straight across the street towards a couple of old pine trees standing by the sidewalk. A car coming up Main Street towards the intersection drove right through him. He didn't flinch and only barely noticed its passage. His focus was completely on the trees.

He didn't slow his pace when he reached the trees. He fully expected to be brought to an abrupt stop when he reached them, but instead carried right on through as if they weren't there.

He stopped and turned around to confirm that he had indeed passed through them, and retraced his steps to confirm. Again, he passed through.

On the sidewalk he turned again towards the trees and shook his head, "This morning trees were as solid as solid could be, but now I can walk through walls."

He reached his hand out to the tree and as expected, it stopped when it felt the firmness of the trunk. He shook his head again, "Okay, well that is truly weird. This is going to take a little getting used to."

He pulled his hand back again and moved back towards the tree again, and this time it passed into the tree unhindered. Pulling it back, he tried to determine what the difference was in the two tries. Clearly there was a difference, but what was it? Could it be as simple as will?

He turned again and crossed the street to the Visitor Center. Standing in front of the glass doors again, his reflection was not visible. He reached his hand forward and it passed right through the glass. He pulled it back and tried again and this time it stopped at the glass.

He thought he knew what the difference was and he focused and stared at the glass. Suddenly his reflection appeared. He reached out with his hand and it touched the glass solidly. He smiled to himself. On top of everything else, this is the first time in a very long time that he could actually see the way he looked.

He considered his features handsome. He had brown hair and rich blue eyes. His frame looked strong, and slender. It could even be considered athletic. Zane smiled approvingly at his appearance, and chuckled, "It is good I approve because I am pretty much stuck with it."

He turned again and started across the street to test the trees again. This time a car that approached suddenly slammed on its brakes and squealed to a halt inches from Zane. The man behind the wheel yelled, "Watch where you're going. I just about killed you."

Zane smiled and waved, "Sorry about that, I must be day dreaming. Thanks for not killing me."

When he was clear the car sped off towards the intersection, the driver still muttering obscenities. Zane considered that unplanned experiment a success. He wasn't completely sure how, but he now knew that he had the ability to materialize in the Liberi plane. He was very pleased with that indeed.

Standing in front of the tree he reached out to it and it was solid. He smiled. He concentrated for a moment and tried again. This time his hand passed right through.

He turned again and looked at the glass door across the street. He thought within his own mind that he wanted to be standing there and suddenly he was.

He stood directly in front of the glass doors and he hadn't taken a step from the tree. His grin grew as he looked into the glass door. His reflection was not there and he nodded understanding.

He turned again and looked in both directions of the street to ensure there was no one around. He realized that he had been visible for a few moments and then became invisible. A witness to that would be an inconvenience he could live without, but thankfully no one was in sight. His experiments had gone unseen by Liberi.

Zane was pleased with this new experience and abilities. He wasn't sure if he travelled the distance from the tree to the door without noticing or if the reality of existence on that plane made it possible for the door to come to him in this plane. He shook his head, "Who cares? That was cool."

He started to think about places on the map and all the places he had been when he was growing up. He remembered his favourite beach on Murray Lake and just as suddenly he was standing on the sand beside the lake.

He smiled broadly and sat on the sand, staring across the water. In life, this was one of his favourite times of day. Here, the half light of dusk fell magically on the still water. It was so incredibly peaceful and pleasant. He allowed his mind to wander and remember those days.

The pleasantness of his memories suddenly

ended and was replaced with cascading flashes of images of places and people. The speed they passed through his mind made him dizzy and unstable. He put a hand on the ground to steady himself and focus. Still the images flashed with such intensity he thought he could actually feel their passing.

$Chapter\ 11$

The dizziness passed fairly quickly. A few more seconds passed as he compiled the images to some form of order. He realized what he was seeing was his own death. The thought of that sent a shudder down his spine, but at the same time, it was something he wanted to see. It was something he needed to see. His mind focused and allowed that last day to play out like a movie.

***

It was a pleasant and warm summer's day. Zane was at work and his shift at the diner was coming to an end. Zane's boss approached him; he wasn't smiling. In his hand was an envelope.

Zane saw him and the envelope and had a pretty good idea what was about to happen. His boss put a friendly hand on Zane's shoulder and sighed, "Things are really slowing down as you have noticed, Zane. I have been struggling to keep things going and to keep you working, but I'm afraid I just can't avoid the inevitable any longer. I have to let you go, son. I am sorrier than I can say."

With that he passed the envelope to Zane, "This is your final cheque. I added a bit extra. It isn't much, but it is all I can afford. When things start to pick up again, I will call you. That I promise. Hopefully you will be doing something else and can tell me to forget it." He offered a small smile to Zane.

Zane took the envelope and smiled back at his boss, "Thanks, George. I appreciate that. I will clean up here a bit and then head out."

George shook his head, "Don't worry about it, Zane. I will take care of it. You can take the rest of the shift off."

Zane nodded as he reluctantly removed his apron and left the diner.

Near-by was a small park with a small pond. It was a peaceful place that Zane had enjoyed visiting on many occasions. It was a great place for introspection and relaxation. If there had ever been a time for that, it was now.

Zane made his way to his favorite bench overlooking the pond and sat down. The cheque George had given him was still in his hands. He opened the envelope for the first time and looked at it. He smiled with appreciation. The number on the cheque was half again as much as his usual wage, "Thanks, George", was all he could say.

He folded the cheque and stuffed it into his pocket. The bank would be open for several more hours. Right now he just wanted to sit and reflect, perhaps give some thought to the future.

The future was never something he had cared much about. He was, after all, only twenty-one. There was plenty of time for the future.

However, it was at times like this that the voices from the past rang through his mind, "You can't live like this. You need to get yourself a career and not just a job. You have to start making plans for your future. It will be upon you far faster than you can imagine."

Zane shook his head. How many times had he heard those words, or words on the same vain? Perhaps after all these years, they actually have meaning. He shook his head, "How? How am I supposed to start over now?"

The little voice inside his head spoke, "It is never too late to start. First you must want it, really want it, and then take the first step towards it. The rest will fall in to place as you go. You and only you can take that first step. Do that and the universe will help you the rest of the way."

Zane shook his head as if to silence the voice, and smiled. His little voice was rarely wrong, but unfortunately he didn't listen to it as often as he should.

He leaned back further into the bench and stared out across the pond. He paid no attention to those that walked by and none of them paid attention to him. They were simply people passing by, all with their own stories and problems.

After an hour of sitting in deep contemplation someone sitting down beside him startled Zane. He quickly turned to her and she smiled apologetically for obviously spooking him.

She raised her right hand out towards him and smiled, "Sorry about that. I didn't realize you were so deep in thought. My name is Becky."

He returned her smile and shook her hand, "That's okay. Nice to meet you, I'm Zane."

The warmth and smoothness of her hand shocked Zane. He looked quickly at her face. Her brown eyes were as unnaturally large and warm as a fawn and her dark hair framed her soft white skin like a work of art.

Becky spoke in a tone that was particularly pleasant to Zane's ear, "Zane? That is a name one doesn't hear very often. I like it." Zane chuckled in an attempt to hide how taken-aback he was by her, "I'm glad I have your approval. I would hate to have to change it after all these years."

Becky giggled as she released the handshake and sat back on the bench and looked out over the water, "This is such a beautiful spot. I so love this bench. It gives the absolute best view."

Zane nodded as he regained composure and returned his attention to the pond, "So true. This is my favorite spot too. A great place for reflection and quiet."

Becky chuckled, "Quiet? I guess I shouldn't be talking to you then?"

Zane returned the chuckle, "I mean really. Some people are so rude." He smiled pleasantly, "I don't mind, really. It is nice to share this spot with someone from time to time. Besides, the beauty of this place needs someone more like you than me to grace it."

Becky nodded as if to overlook his flattery, "I bet your girlfriend loves coming here with you."

Zane laughed at her lack of subtlety, "I don't have a girlfriend. I'm a solo act. A recently unemployed solo act as it turns out. Your timing is impeccable."

Becky nodded again, "I see. So that's why you are in such deep thought. I take it this wasn't a development of your choosing?"

"No, it wasn't. It hasn't even been two hours yet. It really sucks."

"No doubt, I have been there myself far too many times. Don't worry though, there's always something else. Things just have a way of working out if you let them."

Zane smiled and nodded, "I have no doubt, but I'm still bummed. It's such a hassle looking for work. Well, I guess there's really no point dwelling on it. It is what it is."

Both sat quietly for a few moments before Becky spoke again. Her voice was unsure, "I know we just met and all. I know it is pretty forward of me. You don't seem like a jerk. What do you say about us going out for a few drinks? We can call it a celebration of freedom from one existence and welcoming the challenge of an unknown future?"

Zane sat quietly as he considered the offer. Common sense told him it would not be a wise decision to go. This was his last pay cheque for possibly a long time. The thought had no sooner entered his mind when he turned back to face Becky, "I think that would fun. What time do you want to go?"

Becky was pleased by his acceptance, "We could go now if you want? We can grab a bite first?"

"Sure. That sounds great. I have to stop by the bank first, though."

Becky smiled, "Of course. No worries. But, before we go anywhere, though, let me just say that this evening is my treat." Zane was about to speak but Becky quickly put up her hand in front of his face, "Don't argue with me. I want to do this."

Zane tried to speak again but Becky held two fingers to his lips, "Shhh, don't argue with me. It's a done deal."

Zane nodded, "Thank you." He chuckled lightly, "I believe this is the first time I have ever been picked up. I've never been wined and dined either.

"I'm not sure what I'm supposed to do on this side of the arrangement. Don't think you can have your way with me just because you buy me dinner. Who am I kidding, of course you could."

Becky and Zane laughed as they stood. Becky shrugged her shoulders and smiled warmly, "This is my first time, too. I guess we'll just have to see how it goes. And don't worry, I won't take advantage of you or force myself on you." The two chuckled again as they walked off towards the main street and Zane's bank.

It was the dinner hour when Becky and Zane entered the pub. This early in the evening it was the after work crowd occupying most of the place. They chose a nice table for two half way through the pub and against the outside wall. It was a good spot to see almost everyone in the place and had easy access to the dance floor for later in the evening.

The server arrived quickly with menus and offered drinks. Zane ordered his favorite domestic beer and Becky ordered a glass of white wine. Zane smiled to himself as he thought, *'a beer drinker and a wine drinker, this could be interesting.'* The server smiled at both of them and left.

The time passed with Zane and Becky enjoying conversation and a simple but satisfying pub meal. Most of the patrons that had been in the place when they arrived were now gone and the evening crowd slowly started filtering in.

There was a notable difference between the two groups. Earlier it was mostly middle aged men dressed in the clothes in which they had spent their work day. Now the patrons were younger, louder, and dressed more stylishly.

Though they continued to trickle in, it was closer to 10:00 PM before the majority started to arrive. By now, Zane and Becky had been drinking for several hours and were well on their way to being intoxicated.

What they hadn't noticed when they first arrived was that it wasn't going to be a dance night with a band, but rather a Karaoke night.

As the crew began to set up the equipment Zane looked to Becky, "I'm not a singer. I won't be going up there." He smiled warmly but fearfully.

Becky returned the smile, "Me neither, but it should be fun just the same."

Zane smiled agreement and the two resumed the conversation they were enjoying. It wasn't long before the first female singers of the evening took the stage. They chose a number by a popular female singer and began belting out their version of the well known tune.

Both Zane and Becky chuckled under their breath. The singers were not good at all, but nonetheless they enjoyed the performance. They admired the girls' courage for getting up on stage, no matter how much alcohol the performers had consumed.

Several performances began and concluded, all being much the same as the first. There was little question as to how much Zane and Becky enjoyed the shows. Chuckling quietly, Zane excused himself before heading to the opposite side of the bar and the restrooms.

Zane's mood hadn't faltered as he made his way back to his table. To his surprise there were three men sitting at the table and Becky was sitting on the knee of one of them. As Zane grew closer it was clear that it wasn't her wish to be on the man's knee and she wanted off.

Zane kept smiling as he approached his table. Out of the corner of his eye he saw the bouncer leaning against the bar. The bouncer turned his attention to Zane as he approached his table. Zane nodded to the bouncer, indicating he would like some help with the men at his table. The bouncer didn't move.

Upon reaching the table, Zane positioned himself in a way that kept him out of reach of any of the men at the table, "Hey guys, what's up? It doesn't look like my friend is enjoying her new seat."

The one holding Becky looked at Zane. His face virtually expressionless, "What's it to you?"

Zane chuckled pleasantly, "She's my date. I would be grateful if you would please release her."

The man laughed, "Indeed, my apologies my good man." He opened his arms and Becky quickly stood away from him and moved behind Zane. She put one hand on his. She pulled gently in a manner that suggested she wanted to leave the bar.

Zane's attention remained on the man, and his voice remained calm, "Thank you. May I buy you gentlemen a drink?"

The man's expression remained emotionless as he spoke, "Piss off."

Zane nodded amiably and turned from the table and headed towards the bar with the intent of clearing their tab and leaving. Becky arrived first and smiled back at Zane, "I told you, this is my treat. Thank you for back there, by the way. Those guys are real creeps."

Zane smiled, "Sometimes you just have to be pleasant to people and most problems can be solved. And thank you."

Once the transaction completed they turned to leave and noticed the three were no longer at their table. Zane scanned the bar quickly, but they were nowhere to be seen.

The bouncer spoke matter-of-factly, "They went out the front door. I would suggest you go out that door." The bouncer pointed to the door at the opposite end of the bar.

Zane and Becky smiled and headed in the direction he had suggested. Before they had reached that door Zane stopped, "Listen, Becky, we can go if you wish, but they are gone now. We could just stay and enjoy the rest of our evening. You know - if you want."

Becky considered his words for a moment then shook her head, "No. I think we should go. The mood has been spoiled and frankly I feel like I could use a shower." She smiled pleasantly, and

Zane returned the smile. "No problem, Becky. Let's go."

Leaving the bar they took a quick look around to confirm their bearings and started walking towards the park where they had met earlier in the day.

The streets are never quiet, not even at this time of night. That is one of the inherent realities of city life. It is nice to be able to walk at night and know there are people all around. The vibe of the city has a life all its own.

A few blocks away from the park all the concerns of the earlier conflict were gone. They now walked arm in arm down the street laughing, talking, and simply enjoying their time together. Their level of inebriation wasn't high. It was certainly not high enough to cause worrisome attention from anyone passing by.

Suddenly, Zane felt a hard impact at the back of his head. It wasn't sufficient to knock him down, but it was sufficient enough get his attention and make him spin around. In front of Zane was one of the three men from the bar.

After Zane's initial surprise, he wondered where the other two were. He turned back around and took Becky by the arm and hurried off in their original direction. They didn't make it very far when a second man appeared in front of them.

Zane looked back over his shoulder to see the first man still coming. Zane looked into the street. There were cars on the road, but he was prepared to risk it. With Becky's arm in his grasp he turned, "Come on, this way."

They ran off across the street. One car squealed to a halt just short of hitting them. The two men joined together and ran after Becky and Zane. Zane couldn't understand why they were being chased, but was certain they needed to escape.

Zane and Becky rounded a street corner with still a sizable lead on their pursuers. A few feet up the road they spotted an alley and ran in.

There was a dumpster a few feet in with a stack of boxes beside it. The two scurried behind the boxes to hole up out of sight. The alley was sufficiently dark to prevent them from being easily found.

They could hear the two men stopping at the entrance to the alley, "Where did they go?"

There was silence for a few moments, then, "They must have gone up here."

The two walked into the shadows slowly. Zane and Becky could hear their approaching foot falls. When it was clear the men were only a few feet away from them there was the sound of a loud crash followed by the sound of one very angry cat.

The first man swore, "Crap. Get outta here cat." He looked quickly to his friend, "You see that. The damn thing attacked me."

The second man laughed, "Ya. Funny!" he paused for a moment, "Ah, they aren't down here. Let's go."

Zane waited until the sound of their feet was gone and he turned to Becky, "Who are those guys? Do you know them?"

Becky shook her head, "I swear I have never seen them before tonight. Wackos."

Zane nodded agreement. The smell of the dumpster grew in their consciousness. Fear had blocked that fragrance earlier, but now, it was almost too much to bear.

"Come on, Becky, we have to get out of here."

Becky nodded agreement and the two stood slowly, the whole while watching the entrance of the alley to be sure the two men were gone. Satisfied, they stepped out from behind the dumpster and slowly made their way towards the street.

They hadn't moved more than a couple of

feet when Zane felt a sharp pain in his back just below his ribs. It was sufficient to drop him to his knees. He gasped for air as he reached his hand around to his back and brought it forward. His hand was covered in blood. It was then he realized he had just been stabbed and he turned around as he regained his feet.

In front of him was the larger man from the bar. Behind him, he could hear the other two laughing as they returned to the alley. Zane looked to Becky, "Run!"

Before she could move, the two took hold of her and turned her around to face Zane. One of them spoke in an unpleasantly gloating voice, "You don't want to miss this, my dear."

Becky's eyes grew large as the large man thrust his blade forward again and penetrated Zane just below the center of his ribs. As he did he stepped forward and grabbed Zane by the throat, preventing him from falling.

He looked Zane in the eye, "You don't screw with me, my friend. Your lady and me is gonna have a great time tonight. Too bad you ain't gonna be around to see it."

The large man twisted the blade before pulling it out of Zane and pushed him backwards. Zane stumbled backwards three steps before falling to the ground. Life slowly left him as he lay bleeding out in the middle of the alley.

Moments later Zane was looking downwards at his own body, the three men and Becky. He rose slowly away from his body as he watched the three dragging Becky kicking and screaming further into the alley. Before Zane could see what they were doing, he felt a strong pull and everything around him turned to a warm bright light.

***

Zane fought hard to keep his memory going, but try as he might he could not recall what had happened to Becky. He was sure it wasn't good, but he couldn't see it. However, the images of his three assailants were picture clear in his mind. The desire to find them was stronger as was his desire to learn what had become of Becky.

Zane stood up and stared out across the lake. The dusk of this day had passed, and the stars now reflected off the face of the still water. As calm as this scene was, it couldn't calm the turbulence within him.

He focused on his home town and the area where he had met Becky. He wanted to find her or at least find out what had happened to her.

As quickly as the thoughts of that place

entered his mind, he found himself standing in that very alley. He stood silently as he looked around. There were no physical signs of what had happened there, but his memory replayed it all again.

He shook his head to clear it before walking out of the alley and onto the street. The night wasn't much different than that night. In his mind, he could hardly tell the difference.

Now that he was here, he needed to figure out what he must do to get the information he wanted. He walked up the street, unconsciously retracing the steps of that night. Only a few feet away he could see a couple of people running down the sidewalk, hesitating and then racing across the street.

Seconds passed before he realized what he was seeing was himself and Becky running. He was certain he was witnessing a re-enactment of the night he died. Anger boiled in him as he and Becky ran past and down the street. He knew where they are going and follows.

When they reached the alley he positioned himself near the entrance as he and Becky hid. The first two men stop for a few moments before entering the alley. As they move forward, Zane readies himself.

He is determined to use his knowledge to exact his revenge. When they came closer, Zane focused and a sword appeared in his hands. He smiled quickly as he thrust the blade towards the first of the two men.

From the experiments only a short time ago, he knew he would deliver death blows to these men. Zane was stunned when he saw that he was having no effect on them. It wasn't working. He focused and tried again. Still his attacks were useless. Shock consumed him as he turned to face further back into the alley.

Zane watched as the two men do their half hearted check and then watched as the alley cat leaped from the dumpster towards them. Then he watched as the two turned and headed out of the alley.

Zane turned back towards the dumpster as he and Becky stepped out from behind it. He saw the approach of the third man and Zane rushed to head him off. He tossed the sword aside and it vanished before hitting the ground. A split second later a spear appeared in his grip. He positioned the new weapon and lunged it forward all in one motion. As with the first two men, the attack was useless. He and his weapon passed through the third man completely unnoticed.

Zane shook his head angrily as he turned

around. Before his eyes he watched as the large man stabbed him to death. Zane felt sick as he watched the events of his death unfold.

He focused on his fallen body for a few moments before realizing Becky was being taken further into the alley. He turned away from himself and followed them into the deeper darkness.

What he witnessed over the next while made him feel ill and drove him to fuller rage. He lashed all he had out towards the three men with the same effect as earlier. He was helpless as he watched Becky being beaten and raped repeatedly before finally and mercifully being killed.

The three men laughed together as they rose, righted themselves, and headed out of the alley. Becky's body was left in a pathetic heap against one wall. She had been used and discarded like garbage. She almost didn't look human laying there and Zane openly wept.

He had barely known her, but it was the combination of the feelings that were developing for her added to the plain civilized human disgust at how brutally she had been utterly destroyed.

The one thing that angered him more than anything else was how he had been so powerless to help. After all the training and all the tests, in a time of need, he was unable to affect any change to this history.

He looked skyward and half screamed, "Dominus, are you there? I want to talk to you. Why wasn't I allowed to intervene? Why could I not save them?"

There was nothing but silence and it infuriated him further, "Dominus! Answer me!"

The silence continued and Zane dropped to his knees beside Becky's body. He reached his hand out to her, but was unable to touch her. He tried again without success. All he could think was, "Why?"

Then his mind calmed and the scene vanished and he found himself kneeling on the beach of the lake once again. He looked around confused for a few moments before he realized what had happened.

He hadn't actually been there that night. The past minutes were all in his mind. He had been allowed to witness the answer to the question of what had happened to Becky. That was all he had been allowed. As sickened as he was by that, he was equally grateful.

If nothing else, at least now he knew that answer and also knew that there had truly been nothing he could have done to affect the outcome.

The answer, however, reinforced his resolve and the desire to find those three men and exact his revenge and avenge Becky. Right or wrong, he would find them.

Chapter 12

Zane lay on his side in the sand and stared out into the lake. He didn't need sleep, or food or any of the things the Liberi required. But right now, he wished he could sleep. Not for the rejuvenation of his body, but more for the passing of time.

In the time it takes to blink, the sun rose over the lake. The entire night had past in an instant. Zane sat up and watched the change of colors from the cast of night, through the growing dawn, and on to the brightness of day.

He realized that he must have slept, or at least some version of sleep. He recalled everything he had experienced the night before, and yet felt refreshed and relaxed. He was prepared to continue on with a calmer demeanor.

Even in this context, the things of the past are the things that make and shape ones' future. As much as his past had some disgusting memories, they were nonetheless his memories and he chose to embrace them and draw strength from them.

Standing, he took one last look across the lake before willing himself back to Sunnyville. In a moment he was back on the sidewalk by the information center. He took a quick look around before heading back down Main Street. Instead of turning on First, he kept walking until he reached the railroad tracks.

He wasn't really sure where he was going or why, nor did he much care. He just walked and walked. At the tracks he turned left and walked down the middle of the tracks. As he progressed he took the time to admire all the beautiful old homes that stood just beyond the buffer zone on either side of the tracks. The history of the area is carefully preserved in the beauty of these homes.

In the distance, a raised highway delivered the sound of modern traffic that increased as he walked. It was a stark marriage of old world and new. Ahead on the right was a heavily wooded area with some homes intermixed. His destination seemed to lie there.

The last visible road before the elevated highway was where he turned off the tracks. His pace slowed as he continued.

Ahead he could see an older woman standing in front of an old home. She appeared to be looking for something.

When he grew closer he could hear her calling out his name. Her voice wasn't loud. It was barely louder than a whisper but sufficiently loud for him to be sure it was his name she was calling.

Her grey hair was tied in an up-do and she was dressed casually in attire stereotypical of her age.

Zane didn't answer as he continued towards her. She continued looking around and speaking his name. Even when he was mere inches from her, she continued. It was clear she could not see him.

He stared at her for a few moments before curiosity got the best of him, "How do you know my name?"

The woman's mood instantly changed to one of joy as she smiled broadly. Her eyes watered up as she continued looking around. She reached her arms out to try to touch him as she moved in a circle. Zane remained stationary as her outstretched arms passed through him as she turned.

"Where are you? I can't see you. I can hear you, but I can't see you. Show yourself."

Zane looked around for witnesses. No one appeared to be around and he returned his attention to her, "Why would I do that? Who are you? What do you want? How do you know my name?"

The woman lowered her arms and nodded her head in anxious excitement, "I knew you would come. He said you would come." She stepped backwards and turned towards the house, "Come. Come inside. I want to talk to you."

Zane held his ground as the woman scurried to the front of the house, up the stairs to the porch and through the front door. Zane shook his head, but eventually followed her inside.

He didn't allow the hard structures of the house to get in his way. He simply followed the shortest path through whatever he encountered and entered the house.

Once inside, Zane looked around at the parts of the home that were readily visible. It was certainly an older home, with all the beautiful characteristic of an era where detail and charm was an expected ingredient in home construction.

He liked the look of it, the way it was decorated and how well it had been maintained. Zane spotted the woman and followed her in to a room off the main hall.

In spite of the large size of the room, it only contained a small round table covered in a velvety looking cloth with a large crystal ball sitting on a stand in the middle of it.

A set of four chairs surrounded the table. The walls were painted black and the few decorations in the room appeared to embrace and depict the supernatural.

"Are you here, Zane? Did you follow me?"

Zane nodded cautiously as he materialized in front of her, "Yes. I am here. You will now answer my questions."

Zane's sudden appearance startled her in spite of him being expected. She recovered quickly, smiled broadly, and sat at the table. "Sit. Please, sit. Can I get you something? Would you like a sandwich or perhaps a cup of tea?"

Zane walked around the room casually looking at the decorations. The excitement of this was obvious to him and he knew the offer was a polite courtesy. He faced her and smiled politely and lied, "I would love a cup of tea. Thank you."

She was clearly pleased, "Please make yourself comfortable, Mr. Wilder. I'll be right back."

As she left the room, Zane returned his attention to investigating the art and ornaments more carefully, with genuine interest.

She returned more quickly than he expected. She carried a tray containing a tea pot, two fine china cups with saucers and a fine china plate of cookies and placed it down carefully on the table, "Please come and sit Mr. Wilder."

Zane smiled and nodded. He sat in a chair across the table from the old woman. She moved the cookies to the table and poured the tea. When everything was neatly placed she put the tray aside and sat down.

Zane politely took a couple sips of his tea and replaced the cup to the saucer, "Thank you. It is a very nice tea." He paused momentarily before speaking again, "So what is it that I can do for you? How do you know me?"

It was clear the woman was sorting her thoughts before she spoke. She had hoped he would come to her, but part of her didn't believe it would happen.

"My name is Barbara. Barbara Alexander." She paused as she looked around her own room, "For lack of a better description, I am a medium. I talk to the dead. I talk to people that have crossed over. I help the living with their grief." She returned her attention directly to him, "But I have to say, this is the first time in my life anyone has ever materialized in front of me. I had no idea that was even possible."

Zane had heard of people that claimed to be mediums when he was Liberi, but never actually believed in their abilities. He had always thought there was something slimy in the practice.

He considered it a manipulative exploitation of the grief-stricken. Yet here was

Barbara and she was indeed talking to him and apparently had been talking to someone else who told her to expect him and when.

Zane couldn't help chuckling, "A medium? Really? I find that a little hard to believe."

Barbara smiled, "Yes. I'm sure. The profession does get a bad rap because of all the fakes out there. Believe me, I am the real deal.

"What am I saying, of course you know that, or you wouldn't be here. Why I have this ability I have no idea, but it is very real. I take it very seriously and use it cautiously and with the utmost empathy."

Zane nodded cautiously, "That sounds like a sales pitch to me, but that being what it is, it still doesn't answer why I am here? What can I possibly do for you? Who did you talk to that told you I would come?"

Barbara realized her own excitement was interfering with the reasons for wanting Zane to come. She focused her mind on his questions and spoke honestly, "I don't know his name. He has never told it to me. He is male, that is for sure. I have been talking to him specifically most of my life. He helps me contact those that have passed away, on behalf of my clients.

"Sometimes he tells me what they are

saying, and sometimes they speak to me themselves. I never know which way it is going to happen until it does.

"From what I can tell he is very kind. He has always been very helpful to me and my clients. I have never seen him. He has never presented himself to me as you just have."

Zane searched his mind but couldn't think of anyone that would be so open to Liberi, "How did this man know me? Why did he think that I would or even could help you?"

Barbara bowed her head. Her voice was barely more than a whisper, "I don't know. All I know is that I asked him for help for my son and he said yes.

"He said it would be you that would come to take care of it. I don't know how he knew that or how he managed to get you here. I don't know and frankly, I don't care."

Zane shook his head, "Okay. I will have to look into that and find out more information. I am surprised, however, that any one of us would make such a deal."

Zane decided to let those questions slide for the time being and put his focus on the why, "So who is your son and what exactly am I supposed to do?"

Barbara raised her head again. Tears streamed from her eyes, "You have to help me, please, you have to. His father died years ago. He is all I have. He is in ICU and they don't think he will make it. He doesn't deserve to die. He is a good boy. This should never have happened.

"After all I have done for people, alive and dead, I have never asked for anything for myself. I beg you to help me. I beg you to help my son.

"Please, he is only twenty-two. His whole life is still in front of him. I was promised you would help. He promised you would spare him."

Zane sat back in the chair in confusion, "Spare him? How can I spare him? I don't have that ability. I don't make those decisions. I don't even know who could make that decision, never mind who would have the power to do that."

Barbara reached across the table and took Zane's hands in desperation, "Please, dear God, please. You have to help me. You have to help him. A mother should never out live her child. Please."

Zane shook Barbara's hands free from his abruptly and stood, "I'm sorry. I don't know who you think I am, but you have the wrong person. I am sorry for what happened to your son. I am so sorry anyone would make such a promise to you."

Zane dematerialized and headed out of the house as fast as he was able. He could hear as Barbara's desperate voice called after him. Tears welled up in his eyes, and he didn't understand why. Once free of the house his pace slowed as he made his way back towards the railroad tracks.

At the end of the street, leaning against the last tree before the clearing stood a man Zane had never seen before.

He looked to be a man of similar age to Zane. Of course he could be millennium old for all Zane knew. The man stared at Zane as he made his way up the road.

It was clear to Zane that the man could see him and was waiting for him to arrive. Zane altered his course sufficiently to arrive a few feet from the other man, "Yes? What do you want?"

The other man chuckled, "Having a rough day are you, Zane? I am Socius. I am pleased to meet you. I have heard much about you."

Zane shook his head, "You have heard of me? How? Who could possibly be talking about me? I have never heard of you. What do you want?"

Socius' expression quickly changed and he laughed nervously, "You won't hear about most of us here. You really don't need to know us. We, on the other hand, have heard of you and some of us will be in touch with you over time. At this moment in time, it is my privilege."

Zane shook his head, "Riddles, riddles, riddles. Can no one give me a straight answer about anything?" He sighed lightly.

Socius became instantly serious and cautious. He was clearly afraid of angering Zane. Zane didn't understand why. "I'm sorry, Mr. Wilder. That was rude of me. You are one of the chosen ones, I know. You have powers and abilities beyond the rest of us. You are tasked with the protection of us all, whether Liberi or not. You are a guardian. How could you not know that?"

Zane pretended he knew more than he actually did, "You are correct and it is just as correct that it is irrelevant at the moment. I want to know what you want. Do you know Barbara? Are you the one she was talking about?"

Socius spoke nervously, "I have known Barbara for a very long time. I have been working with her most of her life. She is in need of a rather huge favor that is way beyond my abilities. You are the only one I know of that is in a position to help her."

Socius looked to be about the same age as Zane, but clearly if he has known Barbara that long he is far older than he appears. Zane looked into Socius' eyes and saw his sincerity, "Why are you talking to her in the first place? What possible reason could you have for being in contact with Liberi?"

Socius was silent and introspective for a few moments, "That house was my house. I lived there with my family a very, very long time ago. I was killed in that house. It is my home. I will never leave there.

"I met her when she was a very young child. It didn't take too long before I realized she knew I existed. We became friends. I have been talking to her ever since. Together we have been helping people locally and abroad. I would do almost anything for her. She is my best friend."

Zane nodded his head as if he understood.

Socius spoke again, "Will you help her and her son. They are good people. They deserve to live a long quiet life."

Zane spoke quietly, "I will have to think about it. I am not sure it is something I should do. Everything has a purpose and a reason. I must assume this does as well. I will determine what that purpose is and take the action that is appropriate. Is that clear, Socius? I make no promises."

Socius nodded and dared not pursue it further, "Thank you, Mr. Wilder. I am sure you will do what you can and what you believe to be just. I am around here or at Barbara's house most of the time. I would appreciate it if you could let me know what you decide, either way."

Zane nodded and continued to the railroad tracks and followed them back in the direction from which he had originally come. His focus was unwaveringly forward, refusing to look back.

Zane wanted to get as far as possible from this place as quickly as he could. He needed to contact Dominus. With every passing minute, the number of questions Zane had grew. After he covered a few dozen feet down the track he willed himself back to the park.

Chapter 13

Zane's arrival in the park was routine now and he was wondering if he was coming across as a whiner more than a warrior. He found himself standing facing a baseball game. It looked as though the game was between two teams of twelve year olds.

He nodded and smiled at the kids before turning towards the picnic tables and sat at one that was unoccupied, "Alright, Dominus, I am here and I want some answers. I think there is more to my being here than you have said and I need to know all I am to do."

The silence lasted for a few seconds and then the voice of Dominus was heard, "I have trained you and you have learned well. You know that things aren't always the way they appear. You know how to think through every situation to determine the correct answer.

"I am not going to come and give you all the answers. I am not going to come here all the time and tell you what to do. I haven't got the time or the interest.

"Besides, if I do help you through every little thing that comes up, you will learn nothing. Follow your heart, and follow your training. You will always know what you need to do. Trust yourself as I trust you. Believe me, you wouldn't be here in this position if I didn't think you could handle it."

Zane grew angry, "This position? What is this position? Can't you give me a simple answer to a simple question? What is with the constant riddles?"

"All existence is a riddle, Zane. That, if nothing else, you should have learned by now. I will not give you the answer to this or any other questions like it. I will step in if Liberi are needlessly put at risk, but only then and only sometimes.

"What others call you is not your concern. What others think of you is not your concern. You will take the information you have and take whatever action you believe appropriate. Believe in yourself."

"That isn't good enough, Dominus. You can't play with lives, Liberi or mine, like it is some game. It isn't right!"

There was no response. Zane sat at the picnic table for fifteen minutes and waited, but no response came. He cursed under his breath and went back to the fence and watched the last few innings of the ball game.

When the game ended, a smile came to his face. He suddenly realized that he was looking at the whole situation the wrong way. He was unconsciously thinking as if he was a Liberi that was trapped in this situation.

The ball game, the strategies and the results showed him that he needed to look at the problem from the position he was actually in.

He was no longer a Liberi and he needed to make the full step into completely realizing the implications. According to Dominus, Socius and Ducis, he was of a higher position. He has abilities beyond most others in this existence and well beyond that of the Liberi. The only reason for that is so he could use them to whatever advantage he deemed necessary.

He nodded to himself and instantly willed himself to the closest hospital. Upon arrival he went straight to the directory and located the ICU unit and instantly arrived at that location.

He walked behind the counter at the nurse's station and read the list of patient's names in the various units. He found Alexander quickly. The name listed was Ryan Alexander. It was the only Alexander on the floor.

He nodded with satisfaction as he walked from the nurse's station down the hall to the room that housed Ryan. As he walked through the closed door he saw a young man in the bed. The young man was wrapped heavily in bandages. Myriad hoses and tubes entered and left his body. The sound of the artificial lung pumping gave an alien and almost eerie feel to the room.

Zane walked slowly from the doorway to the side of the bed and looked down at the young man. In spite of all the bandages and bruises Zane recognized him.

Ryan Alexander was the young man who was so badly beaten in the parking lot near the pub. Ryan was the one that was beaten by the men that had killed Zane.

This was far too much of a coincidence for it to actually be a coincidence, "Nothing is the way it appears. All existence is a riddle. It was not a coincidence that those men were in that parking lot. It was not a coincidence that Ryan is a victim of my killers."

Zane stepped away from the bed and sat in the chair beside it. He needed a few moments to process his thoughts. It was obvious there were things at play that are beyond the obvious. Zane stood up and returned to the side of the bed.

Looking down at Ryan, he knew he had to help him. He had to fix this. He knew that somehow Ryan's being here was related to him and perhaps even directly his fault. That being what it was, he had absolutely no idea what he could do about it.

Zane sighed as he put a caring hand on Ryan's chest. Almost immediately, Zane felt energy flow from him into Ryan. The feeling was distinct and not like anything he had ever experienced before. It surprised him but at the same time it felt good.

After a few seconds Zane could see Ryan's life in his own mind. It was a blur of faces, places and sounds, but even so, Zane could see how this man's life had unfolded to this point in time and he could see where his life was going in the future.

Zane smiled, "Ryan has a future."

Suddenly Zane was blasted away from Ryan and he crashed harmlessly on the floor. The process only lasted thirty seconds, but now that it was over Zane knew that whatever had just happened was successful. He stood again and walked back beside Ryan and looked down into his face.

Ryan opened his eyes and looked up at Zane. He was still very weak but he managed to utter a couple words, "Thank you, Zane." He closed his eyes again.

The words caught Zane off guard. He knew he was not visible to Liberi at this moment, and didn't understand how Ryan could see him or how he knew his name.

The nurse that had been checking Ryan's equipment heard his whisper. Her expression changed from casual studiousness to shock and she rushed out of the room towards the nurse's station, "Page the doctor. Mr. Alexander spoke. His vitals are strengthening!"

Zane smiled as he walked out of the room and down the hall. The nurse's station was buzzing with a cacophony from nurses scurrying to get charts, equipment and making the call over the P.A. system. A few steps further down the hallway, Zane vanished from the hospital and reappeared on the railway tracks.

A few dozen yards ahead, Zane could see Socius still leaning against the same tree. He wondered momentarily if Socius ever dressed in anything other than this t-shirt and jeans and whether or not his long hair grew or not. Zane shook his head, "Does he not have something better to be doing?"

Socius watched in anticipation as Zane approached. His anxiety was written all over his face.

When Zane reached him he simply nodded, "It is done. Ryan shall recover fully. He will be none the worse for wear. Physically that is. His mental state is nothing I can control."

Socius smiled broadly and tears welled in his eyes as he gave Zane a full hug, "Thank you, Zane. Thank you. These Liberi are like family to me. Thank you."

When Socius stepped back again, Zane stared at him. A moment passed and of all the thoughts going through Zane's head, the only question he could utter came softly, "Why?"

Socius was confused for a second, but quickly realized what Zane was really asking, "I have no idea. He is a good kid. He has been well brought up. He was good in school and sports. He has a decent enough job. He is a fine, clean cut young man. I have no idea why anyone would want to do this to him. I have no idea whatsoever."

Zane nodded, "I am not sure yet, but I believe I may have something to do with it. The men that did this to him were the same ones that killed me. It is far too much of a coincidence. I will find out why these people have been pulled into my existence."

Socius smiled as if he had only heard part of what Zane had said, "Zane, I can give Barbara the news but I know she would much rather hear it from you. I know she has been worried about what you would decide. I have heard her pray a great many times since Ryan went to hospital and many times since you met with her."

Zane looked into Socius' eyes for a moment, "I find it hard to believe that she prays, Socius. That doesn't seem to be something she would do. Especially considering what she knows of us and especially of you. But yes, Socius, I can tell her."

Socius stared blankly at him, uncertain how to respond. Zane simply smiled as he turned to continue up the road to Barbara's house. He didn't hesitate as he walked up the stairs and through the front door.

Zane materialized in the foyer of the home as he looked around for Barbara. He spoke calmly but loud enough to be heard, "Barbara? It's Zane. I am here."

Barbara slowly entered the foyer from her spiritual room. Her face wore the anxiety of her wait. Her eyes were swollen and red as she looked into Zane's face. She smiled and the look of it brightened her entire appearance, "You have saved him, haven't you? He is going to live isn't he?"

Zane simply nodded affirmation.

Barbara sank to her knees and clenched her hands together as the tears began to flow again. She looked skyward, "Thank you. Thank you. Dear God, thank you." Her voice crackled, "I can't begin to tell you how much this means to me. He is my whole life."

Zane nodded sincerely. He felt a little uncomfortable taking credit for what he had done when Barbara was clearing thanking her God. A change in conversation was necessary. Zane reached forward and helped Barbara back to her feet.

"I would like to know why they did this to your son. Do you have any idea Barbara?"

Barbara slowly wiped the tears from her eyes and cheeks as she tried to compose herself. Standing up straight she stared into Zane's eyes. Her voice was as strong as she was able at the moment, "You. You are the reason, Zane. I am not sure why, but I know it was meant as a message for you."

Zane shook his head, "What are you talking about? Who is trying to send what message to me? Why didn't you tell me this before?"

Barbara sighed, "Come and sit." She turned away from Zane and walked into her spiritual room. Zane hesitated a moment before following her in.

Once both were seated Barbara gathered her thoughts then spoke sincerely, "I didn't say anything when we met because, well frankly, I didn't know. I didn't know until you returned just now."

She brushed the visibly brittle grey hair from her brow and took a deep breath, "Don't tell your friend, but he is not the only one I am in contact with. I don't know why. I have always believed that my only contact to the other side was through him, at least until a few days ago. The day after my son was hurt, to be exact."

Barbara leaned into the table as if she was trying to be sure no one else could hear her. She clasped her hands together and rested on her elbows, "I had a vision. It was the blackest, most vial vision I have ever experienced. I have been doing what I am doing for a very long time and I have seen a great many things I simply can't explain. There have been a great many things that scared even me, but nothing like this."

She shuddered visibly, "Even the thought of it now makes we queasy. I have never seen a face, nor have I heard a name. It is more like a feeling. It was a feeling that things were just wrong. It was like the entire universe was out of sync."

Zane shook his head in confusion, "I am not following you, Barbara. What does that have to do with me?"

Barbara sighed and leaned further in, "I saw your face. I heard your name. Amongst all the chaos in the vision those two things came crystal clear to me. That was what made me ask your friend to find you and bring you here. It was a vision that could have only come from the other side. I know the difference. The fact that it started the day after Ryan went to hospital I knew you were somehow involved."

"Why did you think I could help Ryan?"

Barbara sighed uncontrollably, "Frankly, I didn't. At least not until you arrived. I expected to see or at least feel darkness around you. The vision was about you and it was dark and I assumed you would be the dark force within it.

"I made a lot of assumptions based on that. Some were true and some were not. I was hoping I could plead for my son and you would help him. I absolutely believed that you were responsible."

Zane shook his head in confusion, "If you believed I was the one that made Ryan go to hospital, I would think it was pretty risky hoping I would come and that I would help."

Barbara looked down, "I had to take a shot.

He was going to die. That was inevitable. I had to take a shot that you would come to me and make things right."

Barbara hesitated, "I have no doubt now, Zane, no doubt whatsoever, that all of this has been a means for me to contact you and to tell you that someone or something very evil is looking for you. I am certain the motive for this is not good. It is something very dangerous too. I thought you were the problem, but I know now that you are also in danger."

Zane's brow furrowed, "Who is looking for me? How am I to find them?"

Barbara shook her head and sighed, "I don't know, Zane. Sorry."

Zane nodded, "There must be more in the vision. All of this is for naught if that part of the message isn't there. Think hard. Try to remember."

Barbara searched her memory as she shook her head, "I don't know."

Zane's frustration with Barbara was clear, "Alright. Relax. Tell me everything you saw in the vision. Tell me every little detail. Leave absolutely nothing out. The answer is there, we just have to find it."

Barbara nodded cautiously, "It was very black. There were blues and reds and yellows and greens swirling around in no particular pattern. I saw punctuation of colors that receded and were then followed by more punches of color.

"There were vague shapes, but not defined enough to actually make out what the shapes were. I hear the name *Zane Wilder* quietly repeated over and over. It seems to be in the background or something. I know it was there, of that I am sure, but it was only just there.

"I saw some buildings. I recognized them as local. It was like pictures of places here. Then they went away and I saw a shamrock. It grows, and then starts to bleed. Then a full moon rose over the shamrock. When it was fully above it, the horrific screams of pain, anguish and horror began and continued for a few minutes.

"Everything went black and then the whole vision started over and repeated everything again. It has been repeating in my dreams every night and sometimes in the days too. When you left today, the vision stopped and it has not been back."

Barbara took a deep breath and looked at Zane, "I'm sorry. That is all there is. Truly, there is nothing more. I'm sorry."

Zane nodded politely and spoke quietly, "Thank you, Barbara. That is a lot. I know the answer I need is in that vision. I will figure it out."

Zane rose from the table and started out of the room, "Go see Ryan. He is going to be fine. I know he would like to see you."

Zane smiled gently and turned to leave, but before he took a step he turned back, "Barbara, in the hospital Ryan called me by name. Do you have any idea how he would know my name?"

Barbara looked puzzled and shook her head. Zane smiled and then vanished.

Chapter 14

Zane stood beside the fence looking over his now familiar baseball diamond. There wasn't a game on at the moment, but the serenity of the scene was relaxing. It was a calm that he needed in order to review the things Barbara had told him about her vision. He had no doubts that it was indeed meant as a message for him and what the message was had to be relatively easy to find, or what would be the point of the message.

Zane had no idea why Ryan and Barbara were involved. Neither of them had anything to do with him, yet their lives have now been changed forever. There must be a reason for that too. Somehow both things are related.

As Zane stood in thought, the diamond slowly started to fill with loud children. Clearly a game would be starting soon and the noise of that, while enjoyable, would only serve as a distraction to him now.

Zane smiled and willed himself from the park to the beach by the lake. He needed calm to think things through and the beach was the perfect spot for just that.

He quickly thought that it should have been his choice to begin with rather than the park.

The park was the habit and that was simply why he went there. He now knew that it was the lake that would be his preferred spot going forward.

Zane stretched out on the sand with his fingers interlocked behind his head and looked skyward. The shadows grew longer and longer as the sun made its way across the sky and slowly sank below the horizon. Still, for all the time he laid there, no revelations came to him.

The colors of dusk soon waned and the stars began to appear. The closest and brightest first, then slowly, progressively the rest of the visible stars came into view. He continued to lie there, looking skyward, trying to identify the various constellations he could see.

As the hours passed the moon broke the horizon and began its march across the sky. Zane smiled at the size and brilliance of that earth trapped satellite.

He thought about the many centuries that this exact sight has blessed the evening sky. He thought about all the legends and myths that Liberi have attributed to the passing of the phases of the moon.

Suddenly Zane sat up, still staring at the moon. It wasn't a full moon, but it soon would be. He thought quickly to himself and realized that tomorrow was the actual full moon. Not tonight, but tomorrow.

The relevance of the moon in the vision was clear to him now. If the moon has such literal meaning then perhaps some of the other elements were just as literal. He recalled the rest of the vision as Barbara had told him and in the order she had presented them.

He thought out loud, "The first discernible thing she said was my name. That one is obvious. It was something to do with or about me. Then there were the images of the buildings in town. That too is obvious. The next was the shamrock, and then the full moon rising over the shamrock and it starts to bleed."

Zane shook his head, "A bleeding shamrock? What is that supposed to be? Whatever it is happens just as the full moon rises over it. So whatever it is happens tomorrow evening some time. It is in town, so the only piece of the puzzle is the precise location. The bleeding shamrock is the key to that. Given how literal everything else is, the key is that shamrock."

Zane chuckled as he shook his head. He willed himself back to town and to the parking lot where Ryan had been so brutally beaten.

When he arrived he looked down at the

spot where Ryan had been beaten. The ground was still stained with his blood and Zane nodded knowingly as he looked over his shoulder to the pub.

The sign on the front of the building is hand carved with the words "Owl and Gate". Below the name was an image of an owl sitting on a gate and clenched in its talon is a shamrock.

Zane nodded, "This has to be the place. Ryan's beating was a way for me to know to come here. Something evil will happen here tomorrow night. When the moon rises above that shamrock I will need to be here. I am to be witness or be part of something evil. So be it, tomorrow it is then."

Zane smiled at having finally figured out the message and he strode casually out of the parking lot and into the street. The one thing he continued to dwell on was the evil images Barbara had mentioned.

None of the description that Barbara relayed of that part of the vision made sense, but Zane was satisfied with the information he did have. It was sufficient for him to know where he needed to be and when.

The rest of the details will undoubtedly become apparent. Perhaps that was the intent. A means to get him to this spot without giving too much information as to what was going to transpire.

Zane thought of Ryan again, "It is hard to believe that something would have called for such a brutal beating on a Liberi simply as a vehicle to deliver me a message. There has to be more significance to this than simply that.

"And what is up with using those three men? Ryan's mother is a medium, I get that, but why such a brutal assault on an innocent and by those guys?

"Whoever is sending the message could have simply delivered it to me directly or through Barbara directly. There is no logical reason to involve Ryan? That doesn't make sense to me. I must still be missing something."

Zane was certain that tomorrow night would be a test of some significance for him. He was confident of the abilities he had discovered since arriving. He also knew the Liberi didn't see anything strange in him when he was visible. He looked like any one of the many other people around town.

Both of these facts are good things to know. Such information is undoubtedly going to be important. The Owl and Gate was now only feet away. He smiled as he decided he would like to spend this evening with a few pints and in the company of Liberi on their level.

He concentrated momentarily and several hundred dollars appeared in his hand. He smiled as he pushed the money into his pocket. He walked back into the parking lot and stood beside a dumpster not too far away.

He looked around and when satisfied no one would see him, he materialized. He inspected his garments and was satisfied with his appearance. He confidently walked out of the parking lot to the front door of the Owl and Gate.

Zane entered the large open room and stood quietly just inside the door to allow his eyes to become accustomed to the dark. He had never been here before, so getting a feel for the layout was equally important.

The pub appeared clean and simple in design. It was purely a functional design without much effort going into ambiance. There were few pubs in this town, so the pressure to be special didn't really exist.

There was a dance floor and stage at the far end of the space. To the right was the bar and restrooms. The rest of the space was filled with tables. There were a few patrons seated in groups but it was obvious the evening crowd had not yet arrived. He expected the place would be much fuller later.

A clock hung on the wall at one end of the bar and it read 7:00 PM. Wide screen television sets were mounted in a variety of places around the bar. It was doubtful there was a seat anywhere in the bar that would not be able to see at least one of the screens.

Zane picked a table close to the left side wall. It offered a great view of the whole place, plus a view of a couple of the television screens.

Soon after he sat a smiling young woman carrying a tray approached him. She smiled, "Hi. I'm Wendy. What can I get for you?"

Zane returned the smile, "Zane. I'm Zane. I would love a pint of your draught Lager, please."

Wendy nodded politely and returned to the bar. Moments later she returned with the beer and sat it on the table in front of Zane, "Would you like me to start you a tab, Zane?"

Zane nodded, "Thanks. I expect to be here for a while." He smiled warmly and Wendy returned the smile as she retreated to the bar once again.

Zane picked up the mug and took a drink. The fluid was cool and tasted great. This was the first time he had consumed alcohol since he died.

The thought crossed his mind of what effect alcohol would have on him. He did recall the affects when he was Liberi, but had no idea what would happen to him now and while visible.

He took another long sip of the beer before putting it down on the table. He turned his attention to the hockey game that had just started on one of the television screens.

It was the Leafs versus the Flyers. Zane had been raised as an Eastern boy but the Vancouver Canucks were his favorite team. It had been some time since he had last seen a hockey game, so who was playing right now didn't really matter.

What mattered most to him was watching a game. Zane had lost his need to know what day it was or even what season it was. This was a game he had not seen, so the outcome would be a surprise.

It was clear that many in the bar were hockey fans but not necessarily fans of these two teams. They were however, hockey fans, and those eyes were the ones locked on to the game.

It was summer so it was obviously a rebroadcast but that didn't appear to matter. Even in summer, hockey is a game that is fun to watch, even if it is a rerun.

Zane was feeling a lot more comfortable. It

did affirm to him that if he was going to be among Liberi, he had better ensure he stays acquainted with the dates, seasons, pastimes and cultures. After all, at one time they were all his as well. Dominus had instilled a considerable amount of information within him, but he needed a frame of reference to make sense of it.

Some of the memories that had survived were being catalogued, but he knew there was much more he needed to remember and to put into perspective.

He was certain now that deciding to come here tonight as Liberi was a good decision. And as certain of that as he was he was equally certain Dominus would disagree. He chuckled lightly at that thought.

The hockey game progressed and several beers found their way past Zane's lips. He enjoyed the sharp and full bodied flavor of beer, but considering the amount he had consumed, he felt no effects of the alcohol. Zane was equally grateful and disappointed.

Nonetheless he would continue to enjoy his favorite beverage. He did feel reassured that he was able to drink his beer without the ill effects of doing so.

It was half way through the third period

when two very attractive young women entered the bar. Both appeared to be Zane's age and when they entered the bar they remained just inside the door for a moment as they scanned the crowd.

Both made fleeting eye contact with Zane as they continued further into the bar. Clearly they were analyzing the patrons and perhaps calculating their prospects.

Both were dressed very nicely. The brunette wore a short black dress that plunged as deeply in the front as it did in the back. Her hair was done in an up-do with high heels that accentuated her calves.

The second girl was a slender, shapely blonde. Her dress was full length, and plunged much farther down her back than her front. Like her friend, her hair was done in an up-do. Both women looked amazing and in this bar they looked out of place.

Zane found himself staring at them as they made their way to stools at the bar. He chuckled as he noticed that virtually every other male in the place was as equally entranced as he.

He shook his head lightly and returned his attention to the hockey game. He thought to himself, "Liberi! What are you thinking boy?"

The real surprise to him was in the fact that

he did feel attracted to them in that primal way. He wasn't Liberi any longer and couldn't imagine what possible use emotions of that nature could be.

He had moved on to the next level, supposedly a higher level. He shouldn't be feeling these urges and desires. There was no mistaking his feelings were real.

He recalled all the days since he had arrived in this town. He thought of all the places he had been and all the people he had seen, and he could not remember a single instance of feeling like this.

He quickly realized that he had never been in the Liberi plane while in the presence of women he would consider attractive. The only time he has been visible was with Barbara, and a few males. This was the first time being on this plane and in this type of environment.

Still, he liked the feeling and he was enjoying the beers too. Perhaps the simplest of pleasures could only be enjoyed in this simple form.

He didn't like the egotism such thoughts invoked, but was certain it was simply the way of it. Perhaps that is a simple side effect of being visible to Liberi. One must suffer many of the same weaknesses they do.

He nodded to himself, "Yes. That must be it. Good. I do like the sound of that. I have missed it. I think."

Zane looked around quickly as he realized he had been speaking out loud, quietly, but out loud just the same. Thankfully there was no one seated near him. It was unlikely anyone heard him and it didn't appear that anyone had seen him mumbling to himself either.

He leaned back in his chair and returned his focus to the game. In the time it took to get through his distractions and self indulgence, the game was nearing the end. Only five minutes remained and the Leafs had only managed to score one goal in the first. Zane knew it was impossible for them to mount a comeback, never mind a victory. Still he chose to remain focused on watching the game to the end.

Finally and mercifully that game ended. It was a decidedly dominating game with the Flyers beating the Leafs 7-1. Zane didn't feel the same emotion he would have had it been a Canucks contest, but was satisfied at having watched the game. He smiled as he motioned to Wendy to bring him another beer.

Wendy acknowledged him and his

attention wandered again. He immediately noticed the two young women again and it appeared they were looking at him and chuckling. Their expressions didn't suggest they were laughing at him, though. He smiled and nodded politely in their direction while he maintained eye contact. Then he casually pointed to two empty chairs at his table.

Both looked away from him quickly and Zane smiled. He returned his attention to the television. The sound was off, but the program that was on appeared to be the post game analysis and featured replays. Even without being able to hear what was being said, he watched.

A fresh beer arrived at his table, which he received with a smile and a thank you. Wendy smiled in return and left. Zane rose from the table and made his way to the restroom. The intoxicating effects of the alcohol are clearly not an issue for him, but the liquid volume did need to be dealt with.

As Zane re-entered the bar area his eyes naturally looked towards his table. The two women that had been sitting at the bar were now sitting at his table.

Each had a fresh drink in front of them. Zane took his seat without saying a word. He smiled as he picked up his beer and took a drink from the glass. The two women watched him, expecting to hear some comment from him.

He returned the beer to the table and looked at each in turn before reaching his right hand across the table to the blonde, "I'm Wilder, Zane Wilder."

She smiled and took his hand, "Nice to meet you Wilder, Zane Wilder. I'm Lucas, Katrina Lucas."

She giggled pleasantly and Zane smiled as he switched his attention to the brunette, his hand still out stretched. She took it and with the same warm smile, "I'm Debra. I have a last name too, but you can't have it." She giggled.

Zane smiled, "So you ladies are certainly dressed nicely this evening. Are you celebrating something special?"

Katrina spoke teasingly, "Yes, we are in fact. We are celebrating the night we met Zane Wilder. Oh, and by the way, thanks for the drinks."

Zane belly laughed, "Well, that is certainly something worth celebrating, and you are welcome." He tried to be a little more serious, "No really, something special?"

Debra was less flirty, "No. We just felt like dressing up and coming down here and turn some heads."

Zane nodded, "Mission accomplished to be sure. You have certainly got the boy's attention, and some of the girls too. They are all jealous that you two are sitting here with me."

Both girls laughed and Katrina spoke up, "Nice. I bet you are a real lady killer."

Zane shook his head, "No, can't say I have ever killed a lady."

Katrina shook her head, "Groan."

Zane smiled, "I am surprised that your gentlemen let you out unescorted."

Katrina spoke quickly, "I am solo. No gentleman or non-gentleman for that matter, at least not yet. But the night is young. Debra on the other hand is engaged. Her beau should be here any minute. Nice guy. You will like him."

Zane nodded. He was getting the feeling that Katrina was interested in more than just a verbal sparring partner.

He partly wanted to excuse himself politely and leave. Since he wasn't alive, the possibility of such a relationship was doomed. But a larger part of him wanted to stay, if for no other reason than to see where this would go.

The thought had no sooner entered his mind than a young man their age walked up to the table. He was smiling pleasantly as he leaned forward and kissed Debra on the cheek, "Hi, sorry I'm late."

Debra replied cheerfully, "You're not late. John, this is Zane."

Zane stretched his hand out to John. John looked at it for a moment before he shook it.

Zane spoke sincerely, "The ladies have been teaching me the fine art of sarcasm. Well, mostly Katrina here. Debra has been enjoying watching Katrina win."

John laughed, "Ah, yes, sarcasm is Katrina's middle name. A great sense of humor though."

Zane nodded, "Indeed. It is a pleasure to talk to her. Hopefully she doesn't get too sarcastic and drive me away."

Katrina giggled, "What makes you so sure I don't want to drive you away, Zane Wilder?"

Zane laughed, "I'm pretty sure you wouldn't still be sitting here. I doubt you would hang around if you didn't want to be here."

Katrina smirked, "Maybe all we want is your table."

Zane looked around the bar. He confirmed to himself that this table was strategically the best table in the house. That was the reason he had picked it in the first place.

Zane smiled, "Well, that would make sense. However, I have no intention of giving it up."

Katrina grinned, "I guess we are stuck with each other for the evening then."

Zane feigned a sigh, "I guess. John here looks like a decent person as does Debra, so I'm sure the evening won't be a total loss."

Katrina laughed hard, "Okay. Okay. You win. The winner buys the second winner a drink."

Zane nodded agreement and signaled Wendy's attention. When he was sure he had her attention he motioned a 'round for the table' with his hand.

Wendy smiled pleasantly and walked over to the table. She addressed Zane first, "Another beer, Zane?"

Zane nodded, "Please."

Wendy next gave her attention to the girls, "Rye and soda for you two?"

Both nodded and Wendy looked towards John, "What would you like, sir?"

John smiled and looked at Zane's glass, "I'll have the same as Zane."

Wendy nodded politely and walked to the bar to get the order.

For the rest of the evening the four of them talked and laughed and danced. For Zane, it was by far the most enjoyable evening he could remember having since his death.

He knew this was no longer his reality, and accepted that. At the same time, though, he knew he would be back here in the future. It was too much fun not to repeat.

As the evening wore down and closing time approached, Zane was dreading the thought of parting company with Katrina. He wanted to continue spending time with her. John and Debra had left a half hour ago and it was just the two of them now. "I have been having a great time, Katrina. Are you interested in going for walk, perhaps getting something to eat?"

Katrina laughed, "I take it you aren't from around here. There is nothing open at this time of night, nothing. The day ended long ago."

She chuckled again, "But a walk might be nice. I really don't have anything pressing at the moment."

Zane smiled as the two rose from the table. Zane walked over to the bar and cleared his tab before Katrina and he walked out to the street. "Is there a particular direction you would like to go, Kat?"

Katrina chuckled, "Kat, is it? That is a little presumptuous of you isn't it?"

Zane smiled, "Sorry, Ms. Lucas. It is not my intention to offend."

Katrina smiled, "You didn't. Kat is fine. I usually don't let anyone call me that, but you can. I like how it sounds when you say it." She smiled, turned and started walking.

Zane smiled and walked briskly to catch up to her. He offered his arm and she took it. The two continued laughing and talking. They walked with no particular destination in mind, but after a few minutes of strolling they found themselves in the area of town where the majority of churches were located. There were a few churches scattered around town, but this area had the largest concentration.

As they were walking by one the churches, they noticed a small graveyard adjacent to it. They looked at each other, smiled, and changed their course.

They walked boisterously into the graveyard. The grounds were simple but well maintained. New headstones sat in a small area towards the front but the majority of the headstones were older and further back.

Katrina and Zane wandered through the graveyard stopping at every grave to read the inscriptions. Initially the thought of going in there was a lark but now it was bringing some sad thoughts to Zane's mind.

Some of the birth and death dates on some of the stones were for those that had not lived very long. Zane could identify with those in particular.

Katrina sensed the change in Zane's mood, "Are you okay?" She tightened her grip on his arm.

He smiled lightly as he looked at her, "Oh yeah, I'm fine. Just thinking about how some of these lives had been cut so short. It isn't really fair."

Katrina sighed, "That is life. It is sad. But it is not for us to question. It is the way of things. All we can hope to do is to make the best of the life we have while we have it."

Zane nodded and turned to leave the graveyard.

As they walked a low growl suddenly rose behind them and they both turned around quickly. Thirty feet away was a large furry animal. It looked like a large dog or wolf, but at the same time not.

Its head was low and its yellow teeth were visible in its half open mouth. Drool dripped from its mouth like froth on to the ground. There was no mistaking the intent of the creature. Its slow, precise approach clearly showed an attack strategy forming in its mind.

Katrina looked towards Zane, "You need to go. Now! I got this."

At the same time, Zane yelled, "You need to go. Now! I got this."

As precisely together were their words so were their manifestations. Immediately appearing in Zane's hand was his Gladius, and just as quickly, Katrina changed from being a pretty young woman into a large and ferocious lioness. She roared loudly at the sight of Zane's Gladius.

Chapter 15

Zane and Katrina stared at each other for a moment in surprise, and then slowly stepped apart. The beast in front of them was of greater concern at the moment. Their move to split apart now forced it to make a decision as to which it was going to attack first.

The strategy of Zane and Katrina was clearly to be in a position to defend the other when the beast did make its decision. It was now forced to attack one of them, thus leaving the other available for the counter attack.

The beast walked side to side as it approached trying to decide whom it wanted to start with. Suddenly two bright flashes of light sparked behind the wolf creature.

Immediately out of the flashes leapt two more wolf beasts, one on each side of the first. Zane cursed under his breath and started stepping sideways back towards Katrina while keeping his eyes focused on the three beasts now in front of them.

Katrina saw what Zane was doing and moved back in his direction. As she did, she changed her form again. This time she chose a two headed dragon and rose on her back haunches.

She stood fifteen feet tall. Her arms were disproportionately long for her body and were tipped with razor sharp claws.

Zane took a double look at her with initial surprise followed quickly by a large smile. He was just as startled by this change as he had been the first time. He shook his head lightly, "You and I are going have to do some talking if we survive this."

Katrina turned one of her heads towards Zane and nodded as flames shot from her other mouth.

The three wolves continued forward slowly in the spear tip formation. As they became closer all three stood up on their back legs. Clearly they were just as comfortable upright as they were on all fours. Zane realized what it was they were looking at. It was a memory he recalled from stories in his Liberi youth, "Werewolves!"

The formation broke up with one werewolf altering its path and heading towards Zane. The beast's brow was creased, and its lips curled up to expose its rather large teeth. The drool that dripped from its mouth increased the more it growled. It was the very visual epitome of savage bloodlust.

The other two attacked Katrina. Both took

the air when they were only a few feet from her, with each lunging towards the neck of each head. Katrina swung both arms at the werewolves but her timing was off. Both made it past her defense and latched onto her necks. The force of their arrival knocked her off balance and she fell backwards and both werewolves rode her to the ground.

Zane caught the sight of her falling through his periphery. It was sufficient a distraction for his adversary to take advantage and leap at him. Zane's timing was off too, but he managed to recover quickly enough to step sideways.

The airborne wolf didn't miss by much as it flew past him and crashed headlong into a headstone. The force of the impact stunned it momentarily.

Zane smiled and turned his attention immediately to Katrina. Her two werewolves were still on her. She had managed to get each by the throat, but it was all she could do to simply hold them at bay. She had at least managed to get their fangs off her necks, but she still struggled for position under their weight.

Zane rushed over and plunged his gladius through the ribs of the first one he came to. It reared its head and roared in agony. Zane's blade had entered the beast in the precise location its heart should be.

He allowed half the length of the blade to penetrate the beast before pulling it back out. The rage and adrenaline that pulsed through the werewolf gave it the strength to turn its attention from Katrina and focus on Zane.

It lunged towards Zane. The distance between them was only a couple feet, but it was enough for Zane to swing his gladius in an arc.

The glade caught the werewolf just behind the skull. The wound it created opened wide and blood poured freely from it. The beast whined its discomfort.

The force of Zane's blow had deflected its attack, but not quite enough. The rear quarter of the beast made contact with Zane and knocked him from his feet. He hit the ground hard, and was pinned under the weight of the beast. It was far heavier then he would have imagined and he was having serious difficulty freeing himself.

The first creature had recovered and saw Zane's distress. It looked at the body of the beast that now lay motionless on top of Zane and roared its anger as it leapt towards him. Zane's sword was in his hand, but that arm was pinned under the werewolf and Zane struggled to free it.

Suddenly the werewolf that was fighting

with Katrina, flew chaotically through the air and struck the other werewolf in flight and the two crashed harmlessly to the ground five feet from Zane's head.

An instant later the werewolf that pinned Zane was pulled away from him and tossed easily aside. Zane watched as its lifeless body flopped unceremoniously in a heap and then vanish.

Relieved, Zane looked up at what he was expecting to be a two headed dragon. Instead, standing over him was large, extremely hairy humanoid form.

He shook his head quickly and then smiled as he rolled and stood all in one motion. He looked at Katrina again, "Pretty."

Zane chuckled lightly. Katrina looked back at him and growled obvious displeasure.

The two werewolves collected themselves and stood upright, ready for their next assault. Zane and Katrina moved sideways, allowing the space between them to grow. The two werewolves split up as well and circled away from each other.

The werewolves moved slowly and deliberately. Their patience and calculated movements were surprising. They moved side to side slowly, never moving more than a couple feet off the center path, until each was within ten feet of Zane and Katrina.

Zane and Katrina had moved carefully trying to keep their respective foe in front of them. As they moved, however, they ended up standing back touching back.

Zane willed another Gladius for his free hand. Two swords were better than one, he reasoned. As it appeared in his grip, Zane stepped forward a couple steps. He wanted to put a little distance between him and Katrina while also closing the gap between him and his werewolf.

The loud snarling growl of a werewolf roared from behind him. It startled him momentarily and he glanced over his shoulder. This was the break his werewolf wanted and it flung itself towards him.

Zane caught its motion in his periphery and dropped to his knees. His werewolf had targeted his pounce to an upright victim. With Zane on his knees, the werewolf's trajectory was too high.

It flailed in the air as it tried to adapt its course, but as it grew closer, Zane lunged forward and upwards with both Gladius. As each entered the wolf on opposite sides of its ribcage, Zane twisted and released his grip on the swords.

The werewolf howled in agony and grew

silent as it hit the ground harmlessly away from Zane. Zane spun quickly to see what was happening behind him. Katrina had her werewolf by the throat with one hand and was punching it in the ribs with her free hand.

The wolf was squirming and clawing at the air with all four of its appendages. Katrina then tossed the werewolf to the side and it tumbled across the ground until it rolled on to its four legs.

Zane looked back to where his wolf had landed. He caught one last glimpse of it as it vanished from sight.

Katrina's werewolf didn't move. It carefully looked towards Zane and Katrina before looking around the area in which they had been fighting.

It became aware that it was the only one left and spoke in a wet growling voice, "Another time, Zane Wilder."

It turned and ran, but it only covered the distance of a few feet before it vanished from view.

Both Katrina and Zane looked for any signs of other threats. The area was once again quiet and serene. It was as though nothing at all had happened. Satisfied, Katrina returned to the form of the human female Zane had been with earlier.

Zane turned towards Katrina and smiled at

seeing her back in this form, "So, Katrina, anything you want to tell me?"

Katrina shook her head and looked puzzled, "No. Why? Is there something you want to tell me?'

Zane belly laughed, "Okay, fair enough. Clearly you aren't a local so what harm could there be? As you have already figured out, I am not Liberi, er, human. At least I'm not anymore. I was at one time. In fact I lived in a city not too far from here."

Katrina smiled, "I knew there was something not quite right about you. So what are you now?"

Zane shook his head lightly, "You thought there was something not right about me? seriously? I thought I was enjoying the evening with some attractive Liberi. It was a trip down memory lane, if you will. Clearly that wasn't the case.

"What I am now is not really important. I am here to defend all that live in this area apparently. What exactly that means I have yet to determine. I have determined however, that you have some really nasty friends."

Katrina responded in anger, "The werewolves you mean? Hey, Zane Wilder, don't blame them on me. I live in peace here. No one comes after me. I am a peace loving person. I live amongst the humans because I have chosen a simple life. It is my choice to live where I want and whatever way I want. Besides, that last one was clearly talking to you."

Zane nodded, "Okay, Katrina, whatever you say. I have no idea who they are either but it is not impossible that I should. I am sorry."

Katrina nodded acceptance.

Zane smiled, "So tell me, where are you from and why did you choose to live here?"

Katrina hesitated before speaking, "I chose to live here because this place is really out of the way. Plus it is peaceful, beautiful and interesting.

"Humans, for the most part, are simple people and the ones I have met around here seem only to be interested in living a quiet life. I wanted that."

Zane nodded, "You are obviously a shape-shifter of some kind and I would really like to know what your real form is? I doubt you look like an attractive Liberi female."

Katrina thought for a moment before she spoke. Her words were very soft, "You would not be able to see my natural form and if you could you wouldn't like it. My people don't actually have a form in the sense you mean. It isn't a form you would understand. We are more like energy than anything else. I chose this form because this is where I am. I chose this particular form because of the immediate acceptance it grants me."

Zane nodded as if he understood, "So the other two in the club tonight, are they like you?"

Katrina shook her head, "No. They are human, or as you call them, Liberi. They have no idea what I am in reality. They have been friends of mine since I came to this town. I live here. I work at a job here and live in my own home just like everyone else around here. This is the life I have chosen."

Katrina paused for a moment, "I have been in this town for two years now. I will allow myself to appear to age as they do. When the time comes, I will move on and start over again in a new place. But frankly, I have not shape-shifted in years. Not for fun and certainly not for battle. Before tonight, I didn't think I would ever have the need to do it again."

Zane felt bad, "I'm sorry about tonight. I had no idea anything like that was going to happen. It wasn't like we just happened on them. It looked like they arrived here with purpose."

Katrina nodded, "This is a very small town

on the 33rd. There are a lot of wild areas around here where they can arrive unnoticed and vanish to other parts of the world.

"I cannot actually remember any of them arriving directly in town. That usually doesn't happen. Quite frankly, this is the first time I have actually seen anything arrive first hand. Like I said, I try to mind my own business."

Zane grew suspicious, "You know far more than you are telling me, don't you. I can see it on your face and hear it in your voice. You are more aware of what happens around the world in spite of what you say. You need to help me. We would be a great team."

Katrina turned away from Zane and started walking towards the gate they had arrived through. She didn't look at Zane as she spoke, "I am tired. I am going home. Perhaps we will meet again some time, though I must say, I hope not. Stay safe."

Zane ran after her, "Whoa up there a second crazy lady."

Katrina was angry as she turned. She saw the smile on Zane's face and softened, "What, Zane? What do you want?"

"We started off great this evening. We were having a great time. We shouldn't let this little incident get in our way. I would really like to spend more time with you."

Katrina shook her head, "Really, this little incident?" She shook her head in anger, "We met and got to know each based on a lie and then this happens. Clearly it is not safe being around you and frankly I like being safe."

Zane laughed, "No you don't."

Katrina was taken aback, "Excuse me? How dare you tell me what I do and do not like."

"You, my dear Ms. Lucas, or whatever your real name is, pretend every day that you are Liberi. At any minute someone could find out the truth about you. That is a risk you are quite happy to take. Don't tell me you like playing it safe. If that were so, you would stay in your real form and be somewhere else. Am I wrong?"

Katrina was growing angry again. She was about to say something, but changed her mind. She turned abruptly from him and as she did she changed into an eagle and flew off towards the main part of town.

Zane shook his head and muttered under his breath, "Women. It doesn't matter what species they are!"

Zane took another quick look around the graveyard before continuing towards the gate. He hadn't gone more than a couple feet when he heard Dominus' unpleasant tone, "What was that all about, Zane? What is wrong with you? You are not Liberi. You were told not to take their form and expose yourself to their lives. Did you think that was a joke? Huh, perhaps you thought I was kidding?"

Zane didn't stop walking, and as he faded out of the Liberi plane, "You were watching me? Don't you have better things to do than follow me around? You saw the fight with the werewolves then?"

"Of course I saw it? While you are new here I will be checking on you from time to time. You cannot become part of the Liberi world. Is that understood?"

Zane was angry, "You saw them and did nothing? We could have been killed."

Dominus spoke with an unwavering tone, "You were never in danger. How else do you think your victory came so easily? I hope they were enough to convince Miss Lucas to stay away from you."

Zane was still angry, "I do not understand why I can't be part of the Liberi world. No, I will not abide by your rules. I am here for whatever reason. I fought a vampire and won.

"Tonight I fought werewolves and won. I am certain I can handle myself. I know the limits and I will not endanger Liberi."

Dominus roared, "The werewolves were a warning to you and to her. They were a reminder of what your true purpose is here."

Zane stopped and looked skyward, "I have mixed with Liberi and no one was hurt. I cannot see one good reason why I should not just exist as I wish. I can still do what I need to do, but I can also enjoy the time I spend here."

The silence that followed was unnatural. Zane felt like all existence simply vanished. Then, before his eyes, the whole world faded from view.

Not only was there absolutely no sound, but there was nothing but complete blackness in his eyes. All of his senses shut down. This was the first time since he arrived that he felt total and complete fear.

The emptiness lasted for quite some time or at least what seemed a long time to Zane. He had no reference to gauge exactly how long he was in that state. Then, as quickly as everything had faded, everything returned and he was in exactly the same spot he had been.

Dominus' voice boomed, "Let there be no mistake Zane, I have the power to remove you from all existence if I so choose. You are here because I want you here. You will remain here as long as I want you to remain here. Is that clear? Disobey me again and what you just experienced will be permanent. Imagine eternity in that void."

Zane was humbled, "I am sorry, Dominus. Not for what I did this evening, as I will probably do it again. I will probably do it many times.

"However, I am sorry for angering you. I plead with you to allow me to exist in my own reality. You have trained me well, I now ask that you also trust me. I know what reality is and I have no delusions of returning to Liberi as one of them and live life as one of them. I know that particular reality is gone for me.

"The fact is that if I am going to be here for them, I must want to be. What better way for me to want to, than to exchange friendships with some of them. Surely even you must know what the commitment of loyalty can do to a soul."

Zane stood still. He was fully expecting to be removed from reality again, or at least to have to endure another unpleasant lecture from Dominus. But there was nothing. He stood in the same spot looking skyward for five full minutes. Not another word was heard from Dominus and reality didn't vanish.

Zane was unsure what it meant, "Is Dominus granting my wish, or has he said all he is going to say on the matter. Have I now received the only warning I will be receiving? If I disobey his words again will there be no discussion? Will I simply cease to exist in any reality?"

He shook his head and continued out of the graveyard. The only thing that made sense was for him to do what he felt in his heart was the 'right thing'. All he needed to do, at this point, was to decide what exactly the 'right thing' was and what he was truly prepared to risk.

Zane walked the streets for hours. The night gave way to the first rays of sunlight and on into daylight. He searched for a phone booth and phone book. These days there are not many of those around. After some time, he did find one and the book was in it.

Scanning the surroundings to be sure he wasn't seen, he materialized in to the Liberi plane and stepped into the phone booth. He opened the book to the L's and searched for Katrina's name.

There was only the one listing and he smiled as he memorized the address. He stepped out of the booth, got his bearings and headed off in the direction of the address. He wasn't sure what he would do when he got there. He just needed to go.

It didn't take long to find the right apartment building. Zane stood on the street in front of the building as he tried to decide what he was going to do next. He confirmed no one was nearby and he faded out of the Liberi plane to avoid detection by anyone, especially Katrina.

It was still early in the morning in spite of the amount of light that was visible. This was Zane's second favorite time of day. It is always so quiet and peaceful. He was determined to stand here and wait for Katrina. When she eventually did come out, he expected he would follow her to work.

He knew what he was doing was paramount to stalking. Under normal circumstances he would be torn as he questioned himself for doing such a thing. There is just something about her that made him prepared to do things he normally wouldn't even consider. He wasn't sure if that was a good thing or not. Thirty minutes passed and still no sign of her.

A voice startled him, "Zane. What are you doing?"

Zane looked in the direction of the voice.

Zane was surprised, "Ducis? More like what are you doing here? I thought you had moved on?"

Ducis nodded, "I did. Dominus summoned me to return. I need to talk to you about what you are planning on doing."

Zane smiled, "And what exactly is it that you all think I am planning on doing?"

Ducis wasn't smiling, "You cannot interact with Liberi. It is a very bad thing. I did many, many years ago. I was considered a God, as were many of those that were here with me at the time. It was a great time for us, however, in the end, it was a huge mistake. I have never forgiven myself for those days. I gave up my own name in shame."

Zane shook his head, "I'm not you, Ducis. I am not on some self-serving quest. Er, well, not on a quest like that. Besides, she isn't Liberi. I don't know where she is from, but she is a shape-shifter. I know someone like that can't be Liberi. I think she would make an excellent partner. She would be a good ally to have. And frankly, I like her in other ways too." He chuckled to himself.

Ducis nodded and allowed a small smile, "I understand, Zane. Really, I do. However, our rules and doctrines have been established because thinking rationally is impossible when you are too close to the situation."

Zane lost his smile, "Are you saying I am being irrational? I connected with Katrina last night. It is the closest I have felt to anyone in a very long time. She has skills and abilities that would be of use to me, and to us."

"As I recall, Zane, she left you standing alone in a graveyard. I'm not one for metaphors, but that one screams *good-bye*."

Zane chuckled and shook his head, "She was having a tantrum. She knows we are good together. I know she wants me to come after her."

Ducis shook his head, "Oh, of course. How silly of me. That is exactly what her actions said." Ducis chuckled, "I don't think so. You are bordering on stalking, my friend."

"Ducis, trust me. That is all I ask of you and all I have asked of Dominus. I am not a stupid person. I know what I am doing. I will know if I am doing the wrong thing. If I do cross that line I know I have what it takes to stop. I will stop. I am not going to jeopardize everything for my own selfishness. You have to believe me. I know what is at stake and I take it very seriously, no matter what you two think."

Ducis remained silent as he considered Zane's comments.

Zane spoke again, "Ducis, trust me. Please, talk to Dominus for me. Convince him to have a little faith in me. Convince him that he is a good trainer and I have been a good student."

Ducis remained silent for a few more moments, "Alright, Zane. Alright, I will trust you, but only for awhile. I will give you a little grace and I will plead your case to Dominus. He is far more reasonable than you give him credit for. However, I can't see you getting more than forty-eight hours at most to show that you and she can be a team."

"Thank you, Ducis. That is all I ask."

Ducis vanished without another word.

Chapter 16

Zane took a deep breath and leaned back against the tree. All he wanted to do now was convince Katrina to be a part of his existence. She was in the Liberi plane and was happy there.

That could prove to be an obstacle. It was also true that if a relationship did develop, that was a situation that could be dealt with later. Zane spoke softly under his breath, "First things first, my man."

The door to the apartment complex opened and out walked Katrina. Zane smiled at the sight of her. He thought her even more attractive in the light of day. He watched her walk from the building to the sidewalk and turn up the road towards town.

Zane crossed the street and took up a pace several feet behind her. He was not in the Liberi plane so was not concerned about her realizing he was following her. He felt comfortable and relaxed as they walked.

Several blocks passed without event. Katrina's pace was casual. She didn't appear to be in a rush to get to work. Suddenly Katrina turned into a tight alleyway between two buildings. Zane was surprised that she would take such a path, but he followed her in.

A few feet from the entrance, Katrina suddenly stopped, spun, and grabbed Zane with both hands and slammed him up against the brick wall. Zane's surprise was temporarily debilitating, "What the... How can you see me?"

The anger on Katrina's face was unmistakable, "Why are you following me? Didn't you get the message last night?"

Zane gathered himself, "I wanted to see you again. I wanted to talk to you. That is all. How can you see me? I am not in your plane."

Katrina chuckled unpleasantly, "And what plane do you think I am in, Wilder. I told you my natural form is pure energy. I exist on a great many levels at one time. Who was that guy you were talking to outside of my building?"

Zane shook his head, "You saw him too? Why didn't you say something?"

"Answer my question, Wilder. Who was he?"

"His name is Ducis. He was my guide when I first arrived here."

"I see. So why was he talking to you now? My guess is that you are in some kind of trouble? Is that it? I would be pleased to hear you were in trouble. You should probably reconsider your actions, no?"

Zane chuckled, "Okay, okay. You made your point. But if I do abide by the rules, then how would we be able to have close times like this. Listen, we are really getting off on the wrong foot here. I am not a stalker. I am not your enemy. I really like you and just wanted to spend more time with you. Believe me, that is all. I was hoping that if you had a little time to cool off after last night's incident, you would give me a second chance."

Katrina released her grip on Zane and stepped backwards, "I'm touched. Clearly you are putting yourself in harm's way or something by being near me. I'm flattered, but your existence and mine cannot work.

"Yes, that is sarcasm, I'm not really flattered. I want peace and that is all. You are not a man of peace. I know that. It is pretty obvious, and I do not want to be a part of your world."

"Like it or not, Katrina, I am a part of your world. I am part of this entire world. I am here to protect it and all those that live upon it, including you. If you love this place as much as you say, I can't understand why you wouldn't want to be part of protecting it?'

Katrina didn't say another word as she

turned away from Zane and walked back to the street and continued on her way. Zane remained in the alley for a few moments. He was disappointed in how that had gone, but there was little else he could do. At least nothing more he could do at the moment. Continuing after her now would only push her further away. That was the last thing he wanted to do.

Zane started out of the alley but only made it two steps when Ducis reappeared in front of him, "I'd say that didn't go quite the way you thought, eh, Zane? Sorry buddy, I was kind of rooting for you. It is a shame you got Dominus all upset for nothing."

Zane snickered, "It is not for nothing. I have not finished. She wants to work with me. She wants to be with me. She is just not ready to admit it yet. She will."

Ducis chuckled as he shook his head, "This is a dangerous path you are walking, Wilder, dangerous indeed. Altogether, how many hours have you been here?" Ducis didn't wait for an answer, "In that short time you have managed to get in trouble with Liberi. You have managed to really tick off a shape-shifting female. You have had a fight with werewolves and you have managed to tick off Dominus. I'm not so sure that alienating everyone around you is a good idea."

He laughed openly.

Zane nodded with a sarcastic smile, "The werewolves don't count, I am know Dominus had something to do with that. As for the rest, it will all work out for the best Ducis. Trust me. Now why don't you go back to wherever it is you have come from and leave me in peace?"

Ducis nodded seriously, "There is nothing that I would like more, Wilder, but I can't. Dominus has assigned me to work with you. He is right on the verge of pulling you. Trust me that would be very bad for you. He is hoping I can get you sorted out. He doesn't want to intervene again, but you know he will, if he feels he has to. He would really rather I fix you. It is not so much for you, but more for all the work he has put into training you." Ducis laughed.

Zane shook his head and flailed his arms, "Fine, whatever. Do whatever it is you must do. I don't care. Just stay out of my way. Now if you don't mind, I'm going to the lake for a swim." With that, Zane vanished.

As soon as Zane was gone, Ducis heard a loud rumble in the sky. His eyes shot skyward immediately, "He is going to be fine. It will all work out. Give him some more time. I am watching him. I will not let things get out of hand."

The sky silenced.

Ducis shook his head and spoke quietly to himself, "I sure hope you know what you are doing, Wilder. Both of our heads are on the line here."

Zane lay on the beach for most of the day and enjoyed the warmth and sunshine. He had materialized into the Liberi plane for the day. He wanted to enjoy the full effects of the sun and not just its illumination. Plus, if Liberi did stumble across him at least they would see that it was a real person making the waves in the lake.

This part of the lake is off the beaten path, so he was able to enjoy the lake in peace. Nonetheless, he didn't want to take any unnecessary risks. If any Liberi wandered by they would see a young man enjoying the lake and wouldn't think anything of it.

Zane chuckled at that thought, "I wonder how many Liberi have come across us over the years and had absolutely no idea what they were looking at. There's a certain satisfaction in that, and also, it is a bit sinister."

He had been in swimming several times throughout the day. He loved swimming and always has. Having the ability to do it now was an extra special treat. Many of the things he had done as Liberi had been taken for granted, but now great joy was taken in even the simplest of pleasures.

He was grateful, at least, to be in a position to be able to do some of those things again. He could easily have gone to some other existence where none of this would be possible.

The sun made its way across the sky and started down towards the horizon. The spectacular colors of dusk began to overtake the blue. He sat on the sand and watched. It is just one more of those simple pleasures. It is so calm and relaxing, it is almost hypnotizing.

Suddenly a rush ran through his body. It felt very much like an anxiety attack and it caused him to sit up straight with concern. He thought, "What is that all about?" Seconds later, "Something is wrong."

He searched his mind and feelings to try and understand what was happening to him. Then he remembered Barbara's vision. He realized he was sitting on the beach when he needed to be back in town.

He dematerialized and willed himself to a spot just down the street from the Owl and Gate. As soon as he arrived he quickly looked the area over to see what, if anything, was not as it should be. Everything appeared to be quiet and in order. Zane shook his head, "It may be quiet now, but that won't last."

The colors of dusk had passed and the blackness of night began to embrace the town.

Zane thought, "The moon will be full tonight and it will be rising in the east an hour from now. I have an hour."

Zane recalled the vision and tried once again to figure out the pieces that were still eluding him. He knew he was supposed to be here in this place. That part was definite. The full moon was also obvious.

"Wait a minute. She said the full moon rose above the shamrock."

He looked over at the sign on the side of the building and to the location of the shamrock. The full moon wouldn't be over the shamrock for several hours. It will actually be closer to ten or eleven o'clock. He had significantly more time than he originally thought.

The rest of the vision still made no sense, but he wasn't prepared to dwell on it any longer. The answer would present itself soon enough. Meanwhile he had time before he would need to be back at the Owl and Gate.

He looked at the pub and considered going

in for a beer. He chuckled lightly before turning away, "That would really annoy Dominus. I really don't think that would be very wise at the moment."

His path took him away from the pub to a more residential part of town. He had no special destination in mind. He simply walked and thought about random things. After a few minutes he realized his course was taking him in the direction of Katrina's apartment building. He continued on as he debated whether to turn and go elsewhere or continue in this direction.

He hadn't yet made a decision when he arrived outside of her building. This time he slipped behind some bushes to prevent being spotted. He stood for a few moments looking at the building.

Then he shook his head and laughed, "What am I doing here? Either I go up and knock on the door or I get out of here. Standing here like this is pathetic."

He had no sooner uttered those words to himself when Katrina emerged from the building and a car pulled up to the curb. A smile shone across her face as she got into the front passenger side of the car.

The driver was an attractive young woman

Katrina's age. It wasn't Debra that he had met the other night, this was someone else. The two sat and talked for a few moments before the car pulled away from the curb and headed down the street.

Zane walked out from behind the bushes and stood on the sidewalk, "Well I guess that makes that decision easy."

Zane turned back in the direction from which he had come. Not having anything to do at the moment of any importance, he just wandered around town. There were still some areas he hadn't seen and thought now was as good a time as any to become familiar with them.

The hours passed surprisingly fast and he was once again on his way to the Owl and Gate. The evening crowd started to grow outside the door as they waited to enter. It appeared to Zane as though it was going to be a lively bunch this evening. He was momentarily disappointed that he wouldn't be amongst them.

Walking past the building he looked into the parking lot. He wasn't looking for anything in particular just looking at an open space instinctively. In the parking lot he saw the car that Katrina was in earlier. A smile lit his face as he turned back to the front of the building.

Zane tried to look through the front

window but the glass was frosted and he was unable to see inside. Without hesitation he walked through the wall and into the bar. He smiled at how easy it is for him to control that ability now.

Once inside he looked around the bar. There were a great many people in the place and some walked right through him as he stood there. He was still not completely comfortable with that. It did give him a start the first few times out of reflex.

It didn't take long for him to spot Katrina and her friend at a table near the front of the club. Zane smiled as he positioned himself in an out of the way spot where he could watch them without being seen. It was also a good spot to watch the rest of the people in the bar. He may have come in to spy on Katrina, but now he is enjoying watching the entire crowd having a good time.

As the evening wore on, a band began to play. The music was loud, but good. It had the effect of raising ones adrenaline. At first only a few young women paired up to dance while the males sat and drank and talked. They, of course, were pretending not to watch the girls. As time wore on male and female couples started taking the floor. Some were couples when they had arrived, but some were now taking the initiative and asking strangers to partner in dance.

Zane stood in his spot and watched the evolution of the evenings mating rituals. He recalled his Liberi days and the fun he had on evenings such as this. Now, looking around the room and watching the antics he couldn't understand why he had spent so much time on such pursuits. He laughed at his now condescending attitude.

The room started becoming fuzzy and hazy in his eyes. He shook his head a few times to try and clear his vision, then tried rubbing his eyes. When the stars cleared, the room was back to its original brightness.

Zane was pleased that whatever had happened cleared up quickly, but the fact that it happened at all concerned him. As he looked around the room to confirm his vision was indeed back to normal, he noticed things were not exactly the way they had been.

Amongst the Liberi, there were other forms and other creatures. He didn't recognize the appearance of any of them. They all seemed to be enjoying the environment without actually interacting with the Liberi. Then he realized they were not on the Liberi plane, but on his plane instead.

He wondered why they suddenly became visible. Where were they before? He answered his own question, "They have always been here. I was unable to see them until now. Why, why was I unable to see them until now?" He looked skyward, "All part of your plan Dominus, no doubt. I take it you decided that this is the time for me to see the big picture and to be able to see the difference between them and us. I get it. Thanks, things are beginning to make a lot more sense to me now."

Seeing all the others in this place pleased him. Aside from Katrina and the werewolves, he hadn't seen any other non-Liberi creatures around. This is the infamous thirty-third parallel after all. He expected there would be creatures of all forms everywhere.

Now he could see that it was indeed that way. He hoped this visibility would remain and he would take time to meet as many as he was able, in time. Not tonight.

His attention returned to Katrina. She appeared to be in the same form as he was used to seeing her. Her friend, too, looked Liberi. He nodded satisfaction at that. There is a comfort in some things being as expected.

Seconds later, Zane noticed a man approaching Katrina and her friend. What caught his attention more was the darker figure following close behind the man. Both figures had their backs to Zane so he was unable to see what the man or the dark figure looked like. He fixed his attention on them. If they were up to anything, he would be ready to interject if needed.

The man sat across from Katrina and her friend, his back still to Zane. Whatever he was saying to them didn't appear to offend them. In fact, they were smiling and giggling to each other as the man continued talking.

A few moments later the three rose and exited through a door at the other end of the establishment. The dark figure was still close behind and never moved more than a foot from the man's back.

Zane was torn as to whether he should mind his own business and stay in the bar or to follow. He would have to stay a safe distance so as not to be noticed by Katrina.

That brought forth another thought, "If she is able to see me, why is she not able to see the dark figure. Or can she see it and she is not concerned. Or she does see it and she is too afraid to draw attention to that fact. That is it. Her friend is following the man who must be an acquaintance or friend of hers. Katrina is tagging along for protection."

Zane shook his head with self-doubt and

walked across the bar to the door. He rationalized the need to follow, just to ensure Katrina was safe even though he knew she was more than capable of take care of herself. He had seen that first hand. But knowing that didn't sway him from his decision.

Once outside he saw the three making their way around the side of the building and heading towards the alley across the street. Zane looked skyward in indecision. He shook his head and started after them. That was when he noticed that the full moon was directly over the sign of the Owl and Gate. A cold shiver raced down his spine, "Was the vision about this? Does it have something to do with Katrina?"

Zane increased his speed as he followed. He now felt it imperative to be closer. Before he had made it fully across the street, he heard horrified screams behind him. He spun quickly to look for the source.

His eyes grew wide as he saw the Owl and Gate aflame. The bar was full of people and the fire grew rapidly, "How? How could it have grown so quickly?"

He looked back into the alley where Katrina had gone. He saw the four standing just inside the entrance. Whatever they were engaged in seemed innocent.

Zane was just about to turn back to the Owl and Gate when his periphery caught two other men racing across the street towards the alley.

Zane recognized them immediately. They were two of the three that had beaten Ryan so badly, the same two of the three that had killed him.

Zane spun his attention back towards Katrina. He could now see the face of the man. It was the third man.

Chapter 17

Rage rose in Zane as he looked back to the alley. A second passed before he realized that the man wasn't looking at him and smiling but rather through him and at the burning building.

Zane yelled loudly, "Katrina! I need your help, now!"

Katrina looked towards Zane and her jaw dropped as she saw him and the burning building. She immediately turned to run from the alley, but the man grabbed her by the arm and held her. She pleaded and fought against him, but he refused to let her go.

Zane could see the anger on her face and he smiled, "Oh man, you made her mad. You are in for a world of hurt."

He turned and rushed back towards the building. He burst through the wall and through flames to the center of the room. Flames were everywhere and spreading quickly. People were screaming and running for their lives, but they were all trapped with no way out.

Zane yelled, "Dominus, I need you now. I need your help. Show me how to deal with this!"

There was silence for a moment before

Dominus responded, "I am sorry, Zane, but we cannot interfere. This is their destiny and we must do nothing to stop it."

"Nonsense, Dominus. You have the power to stop this and save all the lives in here. Why won't you do it?"

Dominus' voice was stern, "What we have the power to do and what we should do are not always the same. You think this harsh? I do as well, but it is the way it has to be. Leave the building. Use your power to help with what is outside."

Zane wore his horror on his face as he looked around the room. Many of the patrons were already dead. Many others were aflame and screaming. There were a few others that still had hope. Those people still had a chance to survive. Zane ran towards them, grabbed two and carried them out of the building. He placed them on the sidewalk before heading back to get more.

However, this time when he reached the wall, it didn't yield. He tried again, nothing. For some unknown reason he was not able to penetrate the wall. He looked skyward, "Dominus, what is going on? Why can't I get through here?"

There was only silence from Dominus. Zane's frustration was interrupted by screaming from behind him. He turned and saw Katrina and her friend in a struggle with the three men.

Zane's brow furrowed as he yelled out to her, "Katrina, why have you not shifted? Defend yourself."

Zane ran across the street into the alley. The memory of Becky's violated and ravaged body filled his mind. Vengeful bloodlust filled his heart. The man from the bar still held Katrina and was trying to drag her further into the alley.

She saw Zane's approach and yelled, "Help us!"

The man looked in the same direction as Katrina but he couldn't see what she was pleading with. He laughed as he returned his attention to Katrina. Zane reached out to grab him by the shoulder, but his hand went right through. He focused and tried again with the same result.

A dark voice spoke from behind him, "Hello, Zane Wilder. I have been expecting you."

Zane spun around. Standing in front of him was Abbadon. He now knew that he was the dark figure that had been following the man in the bar. Anger replaced his surprise, "You? You are responsible for all of this?"

Abbadon laughed, "I am responsible for a great many things. This is only one very small thing. Back when you were Liberi I knew you would be here tonight. Everything has its place in time and space." His laughter echoed off the walls.

Zane shook his head, "Why? What possible reason could you have for this?"

Abbadon only laughed. Zane raised his hand and his Gladius appeared within his grasp.

Abbadon shook his head and laughed again, "Please. Do you honestly think your puny efforts could possibly harm me?"

Zane thought quickly, "I must be of some threat to you or none of this would be necessary. You wouldn't have gone to the trouble of setting this entire night up." Zane was disgusted with what he thought next, "My God, you were responsible for both Becky's and my death?"

Abbadon laughed again, "I wish I could take credit for that, but I'm afraid those circumstances were not my doing. I have simply used them to my advantage. I knew when you did eventually leave Liberi, you would be trained by Dominus. The rest is, as they say, history." He laughed hard again.

Zane strengthened his resolve, "So I am a serious threat to you. You must know more than you have said. You will not survive, Abbadon. I will destroy you." Zane drove his blade forward towards Abbadon. Abbadon rushed his hand through the air as if swatting a fly. He didn't make contact with Zane, but Zane still flew several feet before hitting the ground.

As Zane gathered his feet again, two other creatures appeared beside Abbadon. They were exactly the same in appearance as the one Zane had defeated at his first encounter with Abbadon.

Zane took a ready stance prepared for battle. He glanced over his shoulder and saw the three men getting further away with Katrina and her friend.

Abbadon spoke, "You have a quandary do you not. Stay and fight or chase and rescue. Let me give you a bit more information to help you make your decision. Those men are going to have a lot of fun with those two young ladies. I cannot guarantee the ladies will survive. Actually, I'm pretty sure they won't.

"You should go after them and save them. Only, I have ensured that you cannot harm them unless you materialize and face them as Liberi. Of course, in the Liberi plane you won't be able to see us. We will still be able to see you and we can fight you."

Zane's head snapped back and forth between Abbadon and the other men. Zane stared at Abbadon, "The fire, all of this, just to bring me to battle? You killed all those people for nothing? Why?"

Abbadon smirked, "Call it sibling rivalry if you will. You see, Dominus and I are brothers. I am the good brother of course. We both died on the battlefield together. We rose and were taught by the same man. That was a long time ago.

"Dominus chose to follow in his footsteps. I chose a more, shall we say, entertaining path. I came across this race of beings and admired their killer instinct and moralities.

"They aren't particularly bright, but they do know how to kill. The Liberi know them as Vampire. A cute name, don't you think? They are far too vicious a species for such a cute name. Nonetheless, I am their king as it were. Actually more like their master and they are my pets. I like it.

"As for you, I have control over everything in this area. I even control what you are able to do here, plus I am preventing Dominus from being able to help you. Tonight you will die. That is your destiny. But it doesn't have to be."

Abbadon hesitated as his grin broadened, "You can bring all your training and join me. We can rule the Liberi for all time. I will release the shape-shifter and her friend and reverse the carnage in the pub. It is your decision. Save all or die along with them. What will it be, Zane Wilder?"

Zane shook his head in anger, "It would appear that I am a far bigger threat to you than I know. Dominus must know that." Zane turned away from Abbadon and his pets.

He ran as fast as he was able in the direction the men had taken the girls. Under his breath he spoke quickly, "Ducis, if you can hear me, I could really use a little help here."

Zane was quickly upon the men and he materialized into the Liberi plane. The Gladius he had been carrying vanished from his grip. He shook his head in frustration. The three men saw his approach at the same time.

The man with Katrina spoke loudly, "Where did you come from?"

The words had no sooner come out of his mouth than Zane threw his fist into the face of the man, "I am from somewhere you will never see."

The man lost his grip as he fell away from Katrina. Katrina didn't hesitate to run to assist her friend. As she ran she yelled, "I can't shift. I don't know why. What is going on?"

Zane remained focused on the man on the

ground, "I know Kat. I'll explain later. Slow them up as best you can."

The man on the ground managed to make it to his hands and knees. Zane attacked again and swung a hard kick from the ground upwards into the man's ribs. The sound of his ribs cracking and of the air being forced from his lungs was pleasure to Zane's ears, "Remember me yet. You killed me. You killed Becky. Now, you are going to die."

Zane positioned himself for another kick when he felt a clawed grip on his shoulder. It arrested his forward movement abruptly and started to drag him backwards. Zane lost his balance and fell to the ground on his back. An instant later he felt a heavy impact on the side of his head. There was no question that one of the Abbadon's pets was on him.

Zane couldn't see it, but guessed where it was and threw a punch, and another and another, but none seemed to have any effect. He then felt those same hands wrapping around his throat and squeezing.

Zane had considerable trouble breathing and writhed from side to side to try and break free of the grip. Suddenly Zane felt the grip forced off his neck. He coughed and fought to get his breath as he stood. He nodded knowingly, "Thanks, Ducis. I guess it is safe to assume you made it."

Zane felt two friendly pats on his shoulder. He smiled and turned back to the man. He had also regained his feet. His breathing was heavy and he appeared to be in distress.

Zane laughed, "Bet it really sucks to be you right now."

Zane moved forward and wrapped one hand around the man's throat and lifted him off the ground. He slowly tightened his grip as he stared into the man's eyes. The man grabbed Zane's hand with both of his own and tried to free himself. His legs were kicking wildly. Though his kicks were making contact with Zane, Zane didn't flinch. He continued to tighten his grip. Slowly the fight started leaving the man.

Just then Zane felt a hard blow just below his ribs on the side of the arm that was holding the man. Zane lost his grip and the man fell to the ground as Zane doubled over from the force of the blow.

Zane instinctively looked in the direction the blow seemed to have come from. He was still unable to see any of Abbadon's pets. A hard punch from an unseen fist ripped against the side of his head and he reeled in a lump on the ground. The pain of the blow was significant and Zane fought to stay conscious.

His breathing was very heavy as he stood shakily. As soon as he was erect another blow contacted the other side of his head and sent him flying to the ground again. He groaned in agony. He moved to his knees and looked skyward as he labored to breathe. He knew in his mind that he would not survive another blow. He desperately needed a few moments to gather his strength.

As he sat on his knees breathing he anticipated the next blow. None came. Seconds passed and still nothing, then he felt a friendly pat on his shoulder. Zane smiled gratefully, "Thanks, Ducis. I owe you one."

Zane labored his breathing for a few more seconds before he attempted standing. As he did, he looked to the man he had been fighting and he too was slowly regaining his feet. Zane growled and moved as quickly as he was able to the man.

As soon as he reached him, Zane reached deep inside himself and brought forth enough strength to grab the front and the back of the man's head. He held the position for a second and then twisted his hands hard. There was no mistaking the sound of the man's neck breaking. The lifeless body fell to the ground unceremoniously.

Zane took a few more deep breaths as he looked where Katrina and her friend had gone. He spotted them quickly. The two girls were still struggling with the other two men. Zane hurried to them with one hand holding his ribs. When he reached them, he released the grip on his side. He grabbed both men, one in each hand, and tossed them backwards. Katrina and her friend fell to the ground away from the two stumbling men.

One of the men regained his balance and pulled a gun from his coat. Zane has never been shot and wasn't too sure what would happen. Before he could think further, the weapon discharged and the bullet passed through his mid section. Zane most definitely felt it and a hole opened through his belly. It did not bleed, nor did Zane feel his existence at any risk.

The jaw of the man that shot him dropped. He tossed his weapon aside as he turned to reach for his friend. Helping him to his feet the two started running. Zane walked over to the discarded weapon and picked it up. He carefully aimed at one of the men, "You guys really aren't too bright."

The weapon reported the first shot loudly and the man reeled and fell to the ground. Zane took careful aim at the second man and fired again. It was another perfect shot and that man fell dead. Zane nodded satisfaction as he turned to Katrina, "I will be right back."

Zane shifted back to his own plane. As he focused, he saw Ducis flying through the air. By the stance of one of the Vampires, it was he who had thrown him. On the ground beside it laid the other Vampire. Its head had been removed from its body. Zane chuckled, "I'd say that one is gone."

That was when Zane spotted Abbadon. He was standing back a dozen or so yards from the action watching. The smile on his face was broad and gloating. The other Vampire started running towards the still body of Ducis.

Zane raised his hand and his Gladius appeared in his grip and with one motion he sent it flying through the air. It connected with the back of the Vampires neck just below the skull. The force of the impact knocked the creature to the ground. The smile left Abbadon's face.

Zane ran to the felled Vampire and retrieved his sword. As he withdrew it, the Vampire reached its hand out and grabbed Zane by the ankle.

Zane swung his sword in a wide arch and it connected with the Vampires neck, just below the skull. The head left the body and tumbled away. The grip on Zane's leg tightened. He tried to shake his leg free, but the grip was too strong.

Zane raised his sword again and severed

the arm at the elbow. With his other foot, Zane stood on the dismembered forearm and pulled his trapped leg from the death grip. Once free he spun quickly to Abbadon and without hesitation, raced towards him.

Abbadon chuckled loudly, "Well done, Zane Wilder. Until we meet again..."

Zane yelled to him, "If you are so almighty powerful, fight me yourself. Kill me if you can."

When Zane was within a foot of his sword's tip reaching its target, Abbadon disappeared. Zane almost stumbled as he had been fully expecting an impact and had braced for it. As he regained his balance he quickly looked around. The remains of the two fallen Vampires had disappeared along with Abbadon.

Zane spun slowly, his sword at the ready, ensuring all foes were indeed gone. Zane tossed his sword aside in frustration. The blade vanished before it hit the ground. He turned quickly and raced to Ducis. His body was intact, but it was clear he was no longer in this existence.

Zane bowed his head, "Thank you, my friend. We didn't get much time to get to know each other. For that I am sorry. I think we could have been friends. I hope you travel well and your next existence suits you."

Zane reached his open hand to Ducis' face to close his still open, lifeless eyes. As soon as his hands touched Ducis' skin a surge of energy ran through Zane like a lightning bolt and threw him a dozen feet from Ducis' body.

Zane shook his head as he collected himself, "I forgot about that. That really wakes one up, man oh man."

He shook his head again as he sat up. He looked at Ducis and saw his chest rising and falling. Zane moved back quickly to his side. Ducis is back and within seconds opened his eyes. He coughed as he rolled to his side and sat up.

He took a second to clear his head and focus before looking into Zane's surprised eyes. He smiled, "Zane, you look like you have seen a ghost." Ducis belly laughed.

Zane hesitated a second before joining in. He reached across and gave Ducis a friendly slap on the shoulder, "Welcome back, my friend. Hope you didn't get too far before I pulled you back."

"Nah, I stayed close. I thought you would figure it out soon enough. Guess I just got lucky this time, eh?" He smiled politely at Zane.

Zane shook his head, "No kidding. I had no idea. Glad it worked out. Thank you for showing up when you did. I was pretty much done for."

Ducis laughed, "You sure were. I hope this isn't going to be a regular occurrence. I'm not always going to be here to save your sorry butt."

Zane laughed, "I am thinking it probably is going to be happening on a regular basis. I don't think Abbadon likes me."

Katrina came up behind Zane, "So, you will be right back, is that what you said?"

Zane stood quickly to face her, "Sorry, Katrina. Yes, I was just on my way back." He pointed to the Ducis, "Meet Ducis. He is a friend of mine and he kind of saved me here today."

Katrina smiled, "Hi Ducis. It is nice to meet you. And yes, Zane, I saw him. I saw you too. I was unable to shift, but I was still able to see both planes. An interesting group of acquaintances you two have."

Zane smiled as he recalled the graveyard, "I have a feeling I will be seeing a great many others over time. I saw a greater variety of creatures tonight than I knew existed."

Ducis laughed, "I was wondering how long it would take Dominus to let you see everything. I bet you were thinking how boring this place was. I guess you know better now."

Katrina shook her head, "You didn't know? Maybe now you can see why I try to stay out of everything."

Katrina's friend moved closer to Katrina. She was looking in the same direction as Katrina and had a very puzzled look on her face, "Ah, Kat, who are you talking too? Where did that friend of yours vanish too?"

Katrina turned with a start to face her friend, "Sorry, Stacy. I was just talking to myself. It has sure been a strange night. I don't know where Zane went, but I'm sure we'll be seeing him again. Are you okay?"

Stacy continued to look in the same direction for a few more seconds before nodding her head, "Yeah, I'm fine now. Ah, what are we going to tell the police about all these bodies? What are we going to say about the fire?"

The full impact of all that had happened this evening suddenly came to Stacy. She tried to talk, but dropped to her knees and started weeping, "Katrina, all those people... Are they all dead? So many people killed. Then these three killed right here before our eyes." All color left Stacy's face as she passed out.

Katrina caught Stacy before she hit the ground. Katrina looked back towards Zane, "She's right you know. The brutality tonight was horrific. So many innocent people died in that fire."

Zane nodded compassionately, "This is precisely why Ducis and I, and a few others are here. We are supposed to protect. We did a poor job tonight, but we did save some that would have died otherwise. I will not mourn those that died, but their screams will never leave me. It is that which will drive me on and give me the strength I need."

Ducis smiled proudly, "Finally. Welcome Zane Wilder, welcome. I think Dominus will be proud of you. I think he will be pretty upset with you most of the time, but he will be proud."

Zane laughed openly. Katrina shook her head in anger, "That's it? Do you have no remorse for all those people that have died? Their lives are over!"

Zane stopped smiling and placed both hands on her shoulders. He was pleased that he was once again able to feel across the planes. I know they died, but I also know they are not dead. Yes, they have left the Liberi plane of existence, but they have moved on to another.

"The people here that knew them will miss them and will be very saddened and pained. I do know that. I have far more empathy for the people that are left behind. The dead will continue to exist. Perhaps one day I will be able to tell you how and what I know. But for now, you'll just have to trust me on this."

Zane paused momentarily, "I think the best thing you can do right now is to get Stacy up and take her back by the pub. The emergency response people will be there and she can be properly attended to. The police will be there as well, and you can tell them about these three."

Katrina looked at him sternly, "Are you not coming? You can probably explain things better than me. I still don't really know what happened."

Zane smiled, "Good. That will make you believable and vulnerable. You will be safe. I will come to see you again, Katrina. I really want to be a part of your life and for you to be a part of mine." He smiled confidently, "There is something about you that makes me need to keep trying."

Katrina raised her one free hand and stroked Zane's cheek as she smiled. She suddenly frowned and slapped his face. Then she turned and gathered up Stacy. She was able to bring Stacy to a state close enough to awake so she would be able to assist Katrina in getting her back to the pub.

Ducis stood and placed his hand on Zane's shoulder as he looked at Katrina walking away with Stacy, "Zane, you do realize you are creating a world of hurt for yourself?"

Zane chuckled, "Without a doubt, Ducis, without a doubt. I wouldn't have it any other way."

Ducis smiled as he turned away. He patted Zane on the back as he started to walk, "Walk with me for a bit, Zane. I have a few things to discuss with you."

The tone of his voice was more subdued than Zane would have expected. He nodded agreement and turned to walk with Ducis.

After the two had walked a few dozen yards, Zane spoke softly, "Is there something wrong, Ducis? What have I done?"

Ducis laughed lightly, "Nothing, my friend, at least nothing wrong."

Ducis went silent as they passed the remains of the two men Zane had shot. Both looked at the bodies matter-of-factly as they passed.

Ducis cleared his throat before he spoke, "As you are aware, Zane, a great many things have happened over the last few days. Dominus trained you for a particular function here amongst the Liberi. You were a good student and you learned all you were required to learn and you learned it well. That is important for you to know."

Ducis paused again to gather his thoughts, "Being a student is one thing, applying what you have learned is quite another. One's character and spirit dictate how one will act and react in any given situation. You have shown this night precisely what you are made of, and what kind of person you are."

Ducis paused to allow that to sink in, "Needless to say, Dominus is extremely pleased with his decision and your performance. You even went so far as to flat out disobey him in favor of helping Liberi in distress. That is exactly the qualities he was looking for in you.

"He knows all too well how much grief you will be causing him in the future, but he also knows that your heart and mind prioritize the way they should. His anger is a small price to pay for the rewards you will provide."

Zane smiled broadly, but remained silent. He was half hoping Dominus would have a few things to say directly. The sky was silent, so Zane spoke, "Why are you telling me this and not Dominus?"

Ducis smiled, "He is a tad busy right now. This evening unleashed a carnage that never should have happened. Many Liberi died as a result."

Zane's smile vanished, "Why did he allow that? Why didn't he do something?"

Ducis' pace didn't falter as he continued down the path, "Simply, he couldn't. It wasn't a matter of whether he wanted to do something or not. He simply couldn't. It wasn't within his power to intervene. Frankly, he made an error in underestimating Abaddon's determination and a lot of innocent people lost their lives."

Zane was speechless. He couldn't imagine any situation that Dominus wouldn't be fully prepared for.

Zane spoke quietly, "So what is it he is trying to do exactly?"

Ducis shook his head, "I can't speak of it. At least, I can't speak of it yet. He is attempting to do something that is forbidden. Something that has only ever been attempted once before and it failed miserably and put humanity on a course of self destruction of epic proportions." Ducis hesitated again, "It was something I tried to do many, many years ago. Something I have regretted ever since, and the one thing I will never forgive myself for. Something I have given up my own name and identity for. Something I should have been killed for. I have been here ever since, refusing to leave in hopes of righting those wrongs."

Zane's curiosity piqued, "Oh come on, Ducis. You can't say all that and nothing more. You have to tell me what happened and what is happening."

Ducis shook his head and quickened his pace, "Hopefully very soon. Keep up with me, Zane."

Zane matched Ducis' pace. His focus had been entirely on Ducis and not on his surroundings. He finally looked around and realized he was on the street where the pub used to stand. He looked back at Ducis questioningly.

Ducis could see the look on Zane's face through his periphery and quickened his pace even more. As Zane caught up once again he could see a single tear on Ducis' cheek.

Zane turned his head in the direction Ducis was looking. Ahead of them was the pub. There was smoke still billowing out of it, and the surrounding area was a swarm of people. Emergency vehicles were everywhere and masses of people were scattered throughout. There was wailing and crying and groans, and yells from those working to save what they could.

The sight of the chaos made Zane's heart heavy and saddened him immensely. He spoke so softly it was barely audible, "Is there nothing that can be done? There must be something."

As if on queue there was a sudden, intensely bright flash of light that lit the area for miles around. The power and force of the light could be felt deep within Zane. He was speechless as he looked on not knowing what was happening.

Within the light he began to see forms moving about in a chaotic dance of nonsense, indiscernible shapes moving so fast they appeared to blend together. Then, just as suddenly, the light was gone. The brightness had been so intense that Zane was momentarily blinded in the subdued light of night.

As his vision adapted, before him the scene of disaster was completely gone. The burned out shell of the pub was now whole again. There were people milling about outside and the sounds of the music from within the pub reached his ears. Zane was shocked as he looked to Ducis.

Ducis nodded and smiled, "It worked this time."

Zane spoke, "What worked? What happened here?"

Ducis turned away from the pub and started walking, he took Zane's shoulder as he went, "Come."

Zane followed as he waited for an answer.

Ducis took a deep breath, "Dominus was not pleased with the way some things transpired tonight. He had a need to somehow make it right. He broke one of our biggest rules. He changed the past."

Zane had seen it, but was still not certain what that truly meant, "How can he do that?"

Ducis kept walking a slow steady pace, "As you have learned, time and space are pliable and can be manipulated. Changing the past can be done, but the amount of energy required is immense. If it isn't done exactly right, one can make things far worse than they were before." Ducis paused there, "That was what happened with me. I messed up."

Zane looked sharply at Ducis, "What did you do? What happened?"

Ducis shook his head, "It was millennia ago and no longer matters. I will never speak of it. I am ashamed of myself and have never forgiven myself. This was the risk Dominus took in doing what he just did."

Zane spoke with uncertainty, "So Dominus changed the past. I get it, what is the big deal?"

Ducis smiled, "Let me just say that every Liberi that died this evening is alive and well and will have no memory of what happened. The three men we killed will remain dead. You, me, the shape shifter and all the other non-Liberi that are here will remember what happened."

Ducis paused for a moment, "Dominus allowed you your revenge and will not take that away from you. You avenged Becky as well. Those are things that won't be changed."

Zane shook his head, "How can he make that decision on his own; what things can be changed and what can't. Who does he think he is?"

Ducis nodded, "That is precisely why these things are never supposed to be done. They are selfish in so much as it is one person that decides what will and will not be changed. I no longer have that ability. Most of the things that happen to the Liberi during the normal course of their lives are the things that are supposed happen and we have no right to second guess them."

Zane wanted to argue further but it was Ducis he was talking to and not Dominus. Ducis had some knowledge but that was all. He was not actually apart of this. Zane was certain Dominus would never allow himself to be questioned or second guessed by Zane.

Ducis could see the fight within Zane written on his face and spoke compassionately, "You need to simply accept that those innocents that died tonight were never supposed to die. They were pawns in Abaddon's game. Dominus restored order. That is all. Tomorrow the sun will rise and our battle will have been won and the innocents are alive. That is all that matters."

Zane spoke quietly, "So what about the bodies of those three men in the park? How will that be explained?"

Ducis answered slowly, "They will be discovered. There will be an investigation, but there is no evidence of any kind. The case will close unsolved and that will be the end of it."

Zane nodded and turned away from Ducis. His mind was torn between what happened surrounding the battle and what has now happened. He was pleased at his revenge, and he was pleased that the Liberi were spared. There was no question of that. What really concerned him was the use of such power. Knowing Dominus possessed it was unnerving. It was equally unnerving to know that at one time Ducis also had such power. Zane wondered what power he possessed that he was not yet aware of. Zane worried about what else Dominus or Ducis may do if the mood should strike them.

Zane willed himself to his favorite beach at his favorite lake and sat quietly in the sand.

Tomorrow was a new day. Tomorrow he would see Kat again. Tomorrow.

Other Titles from S.M. Dougan

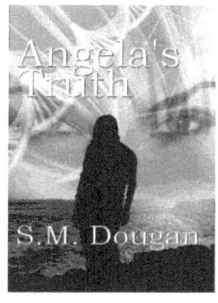

Angela's Truth

Unable to secure her mother's assistance, Angela, in her youthful innocence begins the quest of finding her biological father alone. Unscrupulous computer tech, Dwayne Smythe, is willing to help Angela, for a price. Angela becomes the prime suspect in the murder of her newlywed husband. Senior Detective, Sam Davidson, sets out to the find the real killer before Angela becomes his next victim.

Truth and Vengeance

The events of three years ago have left their scars and memories on Angela as a constant reminder of what she had survived. As the news broadcasts fill with reports of a growing number of local murders, those past memories are relived as Angela becomes determined to prevent more killings. When she goes missing, the race is on to find her before she joins the growing list of victims.

Available at Amazon.com or other ebook distributors

http://smdougan.com